THE FOOTPRINTS OF AN AMERICAN SOLDIER

GEORGE MILLS

ISBN: 979-8-88945-426-7 (paperback)
eISBN: 979-8-88945-427-4

Brilliant Books Literary
137 Forest Park Lane Thomasville
North Carolina 27360 USA

Printed in the United States of America

ACKNOWLEDGMENTS

First and foremost, I would like to give thanks unto my Lord thy God, first and foremost, for giving me the ability to use my imagination to write these stories in which I'm sharing with you. I pray that you find them to be funny and interesting to read. I would also like to take this opportunity to thank each and every one, who has supported me as well as encouraged me to continue with my writing.

I like to dedicate this book in memory of the men and women who were in service in the 624th Quartermaster Company.

May you feel God's love upon you as you read this book. With much love, I thank you for reading my stories.

THE FOOTSTEPS OF AN AMERICAN SOLDIER

"**B**EFORE I START MY UNIQUE adventure through my time that I have served with my hometown Unit of Waynesboro, I would like to share a little historical background about the unit. It was back in 1951 on the date of June 30 that the unit became organized and federal recognized as Company A, 750th Tank Battalion (Heavy), being the first unit known unto the citizens of Waynesboro. The historical records that lie in the archives show—"

"Oh, hold on just a minute here, son. Before you go any further, would you like a cup of coffee?"

"Now, John, please don't be interrupting me. You know I'm trying to tell the history of my hometown unit. Hmm, now that you have asked, I do feel I'm going to be needing something stronger than coffee to calm my nerves."

"Oh, really, Son? Now why would you say that?"

"John, you know I get nervous speaking in front of people."

"Son, I don't think by you having something stronger than coffee will help you to pronounce your words correctly in front of this crowd of people. They look like they can eat you alive."

"Now, John, you know that wasn't a very nice thing to say."

"Well, Mary, it's not my fault he's so illiterate that he can't tell his own story."

"Now, John, I ought!"

"No, Ms. Mary, please don't slap him."

"Son, I want this time."

"Thanks, Ms. Mary, for not hitting him."

"You're welcome, son. Now if you don't mind, let's be moving on with your story."

"Well, Ms. Mary, if John hadn't rudely interrupted me, I would had been halfway through. Now as I was saying, the commanding officer was Capt. Elijah Hal Jenkins and the unit administrator warrant officer was Earnest Rudolph Taylor. The unit had the authorized strength of only thirteen solders—one officer, one warrant, and eleven enlisted."

"Hmm, man, now that's a big unit."

"John, why are you interrupting me again?"

"Oh, sorry, but would you like another cup of coffee?"

"No, John. But if you keep interrupting me, I'm going to need something stronger than your coffee. Now as I was saying, on October 17, 1951, came the attachment along with the headquarters and headquarters company, 108th Armored Cavalry Group for training and administrative supervision. On October 7, 1955, the unit was reorganized. This time around, they would become known as Company E, 108th Armored Cavalry, with an authorized strength of only 152 solders (5 officers, 147 enlisted). On April 24, 1959, the unit once again found themselves being reorganized. The unit would become known as the 193rd Transportation Company (Tactical Carry) with an authorized strength of only eighty solders. Being of these eighty-six personnel, there were only three officers, one warrant, and eighty-two enlisted. On February 21, 1961, the unit would receive state active duty orders for Operation Flood Duty to support an assist civil authority in the areas flooded by Chickasawhay River. Their duties consist of evacuating and housing flood refugees, controlling and directing traffic, and restoring and preserving the order to those areas which were affected by the flood. On September 30, 1962, the unit once again would find themselves to be called upon. This time, it would be federal active duty service at their home station. On October 10, 1962, they were revered back to the control of their state.

"Now, Mr. and Mrs. John, if you would just stay with me a little longer, because here's where the good time or where we're about to come alive. On the date of August 1, 1982, the unit will find itself to reorganize once again. Now this time, the unit, however, will become known as the 624th Quarter Master Company."

"The one that some might say I cut my teeth on."

"Hmm, just never mind John. It's an ole Southern saying."

"Now the unit was giving the authorized strength of having 118 solders—3 of them were officers and 1 warrant, which left only 114 enlisted to do the work."

"Wait now, son. Just where do you think you are going?"

"John, I've shared a little of the history behind the unit with you. Now I'm going to get on my motorcycle and ride off into the sunset, and let the rest of the history continue to unfold before your very eyes."

"Son, before you go riding off into the sunset, please let me deeply apologize for John's inappropriate comments earlier. Not everyone sees you as being illiterate. Son, I greatly admire your true Christian walk. There are very few men in this world who can honestly say they have shown the solid Christian picture as you have and do. 'For the fear of the Lord is the beginning of knowledge,' and you do this well."

"Wow, I'm at a loss for words here, Ms. Mary. All I can say is thank you for those kind words."

* * * * *

I hope you'll enjoy the journey as it moves forward from here. For one day, my friend, the journey in which you are about to take on will surely come to an end. May the true blessings of God's love be with you through this long and happy journey. I'm hopeful of seeing you at the end, beginning here or there, in the kingdom of God Almighty.

A NEW NORM BEGINS TO TAKE SHAPE

AFTER READING ROMANS CHAPTER 2, I find myself having a better understanding of the words of our Lord thy God as how I, as a new born-again Christian, should be living a spiritual life here on earth. To honor him as our Savior, who paid the ultimate price—his life—on that unforgettable day. He was nailed to a rugged cross with a crown of thorns placed on his head, having his side pierced with a spear by a Roman soldier. I myself could not have paid this price. Even to this day, I don't understand why there are some people that say they are a born-again Christian, when every other word that comes forth from their mouths, they're taking God's name in vain. For I'm left only to guess that the society of this world in which I have found myself living in today has put God's word on the back burner. Now this appears to have become the new norm and is now accepted as a Christian.

'Son, why would you say this?"

After all, haven't the Ten Commandments and the right to pray been taken out of public schools and all other public places. I remember when praying in school was something we did every morning before starting with our school activities, and no one got offended by doing so. Now if someone even talks about praying in schools, it causes an uproar and becomes offensive. I can't help but wonder why someone would say they're offended by prayer. Can it be because they don't like the guilty feelings of their ungodly, unmolded behavior? For there are people who have no sense of a Christian's belief in God. For God has created us all in his own image. Let's investigate the living words of Jeremiah, where God had this to say:

> Before I formed thee in the belly, I knew thee; and before thou came forth out of the womb, I sanctified thee, and I ordained thee a prophet unto the nations. Then said I, Ah, Lord God! Behold, I cannot speak, for I am a child. But the Lord said unto me; "Say not, I am a child, for thou shalt go to all that I shall send thee, and whatsoever I command thee thou shalt speak. Be not afraid of their faces: for I am with thee to deliver thee," said the Lord. (Jer. 1:5–8, KJV)

Christians could also say they are offended by those who oppose their kids of having the right to pray in school. If you would look at the Ten Commandments, the very first one says, "We should have no other God before the Lord your God."

Though we have took it upon ourselves to let our love of money and other earthly things come before God, who gave his only begotten Son, Jesus. I must ask: how can a nation of people still call itself a "Christian nation," when the people of that nation have let the elected officials pass a law that allow women to have an abortion of their unborn child at any stage of her pregnancy? These people are the same ones who are warning to take away the rights of the people to own a gun. Have these people forgotten that guns are only for the protection of their families and for bringing food unto the table when necessary? Instead, so many people are using them to kill other people because of the ungodly hardness of their heart.

"Let me ask you a hypothetical question here, John. Could this be because the kids had been given everything they have asked for from one generation to generation by their parents? Could it be because they want their kids to have more than they had when they were growing up in a world and have forgotten how to teach them to put God first? I ask, John, does this not sound like a world that has been turned over to a reprobate mind? I remember a time growing up as a young boy going to church, hearing the preacher preach on the Ten Commandments and how we are to live by them. But in today's world, all you hear is, "Sow a seed of a thousand or more dollars and God will surely bless you in ways unlike he had ever blessed you before."

I'm thinking now, "Preacher, you've got to be kidding me, right? I don't have a thousand or more dollars to sow unto you as a seed. Preacher, therefore, I'm guessing now I'll never be blessed by God because of my inability to send you a thousand dollars. I recall this song by Johnny Paycheck, "The Outlaw's Prayer." Just shame, shame on me, Mr. Preacher. Now, Preacher, as I understand the words of God, for it says you are to bring a tenth of your earnings into the storehouse. Let's just look in the book of Malachi and see what is said about tithing. Chapter 3 verse 10:

> Bring ye all the tithes into the storehouse, that there may be met in mine house, and prove me now herewith, saith the Lord of hosts, if I will not open you the windows of heaven, and pour you out a blessing, that there shall not be room enough to receive it. (Mal. 3:10)
>
> But unto you that fear my name shall the Son of righteousness arise with healing in his wings; and ye shall go forth and grow up as calves of the stall. And ye shall tread down the wicked; for they shall be ashes under the soles of your feet in the day that I shall do this, saith the Lord of hosts. (Mal. 4:2–3)

As I find myself starting my new journey once again down this old rugged dirt road we call life, I have come to discover that there are some things that you just can't change. All you can do is put your troubles and lack of understanding of some peoples' ways into the hands of God and let him be your guide. No matter how hard you try to be a great friend to someone, they just can't seem to find it in their own heart as a born-again Christian to forgive you for whatever you may have done. If they are not willing to accept you as you are, then you have just been wasting your valuable time. You need to be moving on with your own life and do the very best you can. Not everyone is going to accept you as a born-again Christian, as they did not accept our Lord Jesus. When Jesus walked the earth, he was teaching people how we should be living our lives. When I find myself face-to-face with someone such as this and knowing that you can't please everyone, I'm reminded of the words Jesus said in Matthew 10:14 and in Mark 6:11. If you will, I would like for you to read these two books in K.JV. If you are reading this and have not yet come to know Jesus as your own personal Savior, I would like for you to find yourself a Holy Bible and start reading and studying it for yourself. I feel you would find it to be one of the best-written books you will ever read, and the greatest book that has ever been written.

Now we find ourselves wondering why there is so much killing of young people in our schools today, and it is not only in schools, but it's also out on the streets as well as in the homes. They have passed a law that says it's okay for a woman to have an abortion of her unborn child. Mr. John, is that not also committing a murder of an innocent life? Why don't they pass a new law to put a stop to that killing? The leaders who are elected to lead want to pass new laws but have taken the most important laws out of the schools and other public places. Until they themselves turn back unto the laws that God has given us to live by. They can put all the new laws that they want into effect, and it will not stop people who are trapped in the ways of the world. For Cain killed his brother Abel with a stone, and in 1 Samuel 17, David hurled a stone from his sling and hit Goliath in the center of his forehead. If you were to read the Holy Bible, you would see that there were people killing other people without any guns. Hearing these things, I'm reminded of the people that Moses led out of Egypt. Do you remember what took place with the people when Moses went up into the mountains to seek God's guidance for the people in those days?

I would like you to look in the book of Exodus chapter 32 and read it for yourself, and then look at how some people are living out their lives. It's as if we are living just as the people did back in those days. I'm going to say goodnight now, and I hold you take the time out of your busy schedule to read these chapters for yourself.

* * * * *

As I walked downstairs into the kitchen, I saw Mr. and Mrs. John awake bright and early, getting ready for breakfast. "Good morning, Mr. and Mrs. John. How are you this morning?"

"Oh, son, we are doing okay. Just thankful to be alive to see another beautiful day that God has blessed us with. Would you like for me to fix you some breakfast?" she says in a soft, caring tone.

"Yes, thank you, ma'am. That would be very nice of you."

Mr. John's eyes met mine as if he had been waiting for the moment I stepped downstairs. I knew exactly what he was going to ask of me. "Now, son, while you are waiting on Mrs. John to fix you breakfast, I would like to hear some of your stories when you were growing up, if you don't mind sharing some with us."

I could hear the excitement in his voice. I had no earthly idea my stories were this interesting to others. "Well, John, I guess I can share one or two while I have my coffee." I say with a grin. "Do you remember when I was going to tell you about the morning that my brother and I were on our way home from work?"

"Oh yes, I do. Are you going to tell what took place that morning while the truck was airborne?"

"Only if you don't interrupt by asking questions."

"Okay, son. I will try not to."

"We were on our way home that morning. I was driving about fifty-five miles per hour when we came upon this pile of dirt that the engineers left on the road. I ramped it, and airborne we went. Well, we didn't say anything until we got to his house. That was when I asked him if my spare tire was still in the back. He said, 'No, it's not there. It got slung off when we were airborne.'"

"Son, you were lucky that it didn't come through the back glass."

"Yes, sir. You are right about that. That would not have been good at all now, would it?"

"There was another time when we were on our way home from work. We came up on this person lying in the middle of the road. We didn't know if he was alive or dead."

"Well, what did you all do, Son?"

"Well, John, one of our coworker who had gotten there before us said that someone had went on ahead to call the law. Well, by the time the law arrived, there was a car that came over the hill and nearly ran the person over. I myself got down beside my car. My brother went over the hood of my car. Everyone else ran for safety to keep from being hit by the car as it swerved to keep from hitting the person in the middle of the road."

"What happened to the car? Did it stop or did it keep going?"

"Mrs. John, they ended up in the ditch."

"Did anyone in the car get hurt?"

"No, ma'am. They just asked, 'Why is that person lying in the middle of the road?'"

"Why was this person lying on the road, Son?"

"John, I don't know why. I guess he got sleepy and decided to lie down."

"So, he wasn't dead?"

"No, John. He wasn't dead."

"How do you know he wasn't dead, Son?"

"Because the paramedics said he just passed out from exhaustion."

"What happened next, Son?"

"We all went home. There was nothing else for us to do."

"Did they get the car out of the ditch?"

"Yes, John. We had helped the women get their car out of the ditch."

"Son, can I ask you? Was this your first job out of high school?"

"No, John. When I finished high school, I went to work part time for one of my best friends' father at a sawmill."

"What kind of work did you do?"

"John, you sure like asking questions."

"Son, if I don't ask, how will I know anything?"

"Okay, John. I kept the ground, cutting grass and weed-eating around the place. He had me doing all kinds of odd jobs. There was this one job he had me doing. I had to clean out the sludge pond. My job was to get the suction hose farther out into the pond. When I stepped out to do that, my foot and part of my leg disappeared into the mud. I was stuck! I had already seen a snake swimming around in the pond, and I didn't know exactly where it had gone, so I was clawing at the ground, trying to pull my leg out of the mud. I finally got my leg free and went on to finish the job, and then he had me to clean out from under the scales. Scales, you ask. Oh, the scales are what they weighed the logs with, almost like a paperweight. Over time, bark from off the logs would pile up under the scales and would need to be removed in order to get a true reading of the weight of the logs. By the time I was done with that, it was time to cut the grass and weed-eat again. There was one day I was weed-eating along the railroad tracks when I came across a hive of bumblebees. I started running, and the bumblebees came chasing after me and tore me up! They stung the back of my head, my back, and legs."

"What did you do, Son?"

"What do you mean what did I do? I ran to the shop and had my boss rub alcohol all over my back, that's what I did. Then I went back weed-eating behind the office of one of the other supervisors when the blade of the weed-eater struck a rock, slinging it into the wall of his office! He came running out to see what was going on. The supervisor stopped me and began to tell me he thought someone was shooting up his office! When I was done with the weed-eating for the day, he then put me to work at the stacker, laying eight-foot-long sticks between the rough lumber. The reason for putting sticks between the layers of lumber, you ask. Well, it was for the hot air to flow through and dry the lumber."

"Son, what did they do with the rough lumber after it was dry?"

"Well, they then ran it through a big planner, planning the board down to size. Mr. John, I'm going to take a break here and take a ride on one of your motorcycles. I feel like being alone for a little while just to clear my mind, if that's okay. Before I go, I have a question I would like to ask you."

"Sure, son, go ahead. I don't mind you asking. What's your question?"

"Why would someone find themselves interested in a person who is not in any way interested in them?"

"Well, son, that is a hard question to answer. I'm going to need some time to think about this question."

"Well, before I leave this old desert, do you think that you can give me an answer to such a question as this one?"

"Where are you going, Son?"

"I don't know. I'm just going for a long ride to clear my mind."

"Okay, you just be careful out there, and don't do like you did that one morning on your way to work."

"Oh, you are talking about the time when I was on my 550 Suzuki and my lunch box fell from between my legs? I ended upside down in the ditch with the motorcycle on top of me. That bike does bring back some old memories, but for now, I will just put them on hold and go for a ride. While on my ride, I will reflect in memory to this one October when some of my fellow classmates were holding a fall festival at this old home they decided to decorate as a haunted house. They asked if I would like to participate in the fun, so I agreed, but I had to play the role of the devil. They gave me this red costume to dress up in and had me sit in a dark room by the door. While sitting there, this young girl and boy came in. The girl said, 'It's real!' and the boy said, 'No, it's not. See I will show you.' He stomped my foot, for it was all I could do to stop myself from letting out a scream of my own. Now that I look back on the situation, I should have. But at the time, I didn't want to scare the life out of the young girl. I can imagine seeing that young boy leaving there, running for his life, if I had come up out of the chair screaming at the top of my lungs after he had said, 'See, it's not real.'

"After leaving there, I headed home. It was late, and the store was closed. I didn't need any gas, or so I thought. But about three miles from home, I ran out. I needed to find a gas station and get gas in this one before I continued my long ride back to the shop. While at the store, I saw this small building that reminded me of a time when my younger brother and I had started. We came home early from school one day and it was raining. We were not able to get inside the house for we had forgotten the keys. Mom was gone to take our stepdad some lunch. So we decided, while we waited for Mom to get back, that we would get inside the pump house to get out of the freezing rain. Little did we know that there was one of our stepdad's hens sitting on her eggs. The old hen came up her eggs and attacked us because she was trying to protect her eggs from what she thought was someone trying to take them. Before it was all said and done, we almost tore down the pump house trying to get away from her. Mom finally got home and saw us all beat up and torn from the hen. Mom asked us, 'Have you and your brother been wrestling with each other again?' We replied with, 'No, ma'am. We were just trying to get away from the hen that was in the pump house sitting on her eggs.'"

As I made my way back to the shop, I remembered one night that I had let my brother use my car to go see his girlfriend. I was getting ready for bed when I saw headlights coming through the bedroom window as he came around the curve coming to the house. Oh, I thought it was a good time for payback for what he had done to me earlier that day. I was standing with my hand over the light switch, waiting for him to turn on the light, then I grabbed his hand. Oh yes, I got him. It was a great payback. He let out a scream that got Mom out of bed.

Mom asked, "What is going on in there?"

"Oh, Mom, he just scared the life out of me," he replied.

Mom came back with her only reply, "You two best behave yourself and go bed before I come back there. And you know you don't want me to come in there because you know just what will happen."

"Yes, ma'am. We love you, Mom. Good night."

THE LONG RIDE HOME

Now I WAS BACK TO the shop and Mr. John asked, "How did your ride go, Stash?"

"What did you just call me, Mr. John?"

"Stash is what the lady from the coffee shop called you today when she stopped by to see you. She said for you to come by the store. She wanted to tell you something."

"Okay, did she say anything about what she might wanted to tell me?"

"No, Stash. She didn't say anything other than she needed to see you right away. Well, it was a nice one. It brought back some great memories of my childhood. That is great Stash," he said. "I have put some thought into the question you had asked me earlier. Come on in and get a cup of coffee, and I'll tell you what I came up with."

"Okay. Thanks, Mr. John. Sounds great."

"Here's your coffee, Stash. Now as I was saying about your question earlier, before you went on your ride. Now this may not make any sense to you, but it's the only thing that I could think of. Could it be why you find this person to be interesting is because he or she does not find you to be interesting?"

"Well, Mr. John, I guess that is one way you could look at it. Thank you for the coffee. Now I guess I will walk down to the coffee shop and see what that beautiful lady wanted to see me about."

"Stash, before you go, will you finish telling me about your first job?"

"Well, I guess I could. Now let me see where I stopped in telling that story. Oh yes. I think I was talking about this old building that they used at one time for their break room that they had to abandon because the roof was falling in. He had me to tear it down with a backhoe and then load the scraps onto a dump -truck to haul it to the dump. That's where I learned how to operate a backhoe and drive a dump truck."

"How long did you work at this sawmill, Stash?"

"Oh, until he made me mad one day and I just said, 'Okay, that it's. I'm not going to take any more of this. I have had enough. I'm going to the house."

"Well, Stash, what did he do to make you so mad that you just walked out like that?"

"Well, Mr. John, it's like this. All the other supervisors who worked there was telling me that they had never seen the place look any better, and all he would tell me at the end of the day was what a sorry job I was doing in keeping the place up. One day, while on my lunch break, I decided that I had enough of him telling me this, so I just walked out. I walked about twenty miles that day before I got to a place where I could call my stepdad to come pick me up. Let me say that was a long walk in a pair of steel-toe cowboy boots. The further I walked, the madder I became."

"Stash, now how could you be getting any madder than what you already were?"

"Well, John, the cowboy boots that I had on were beginning to rub blisters on my heels from walking such a long distance."

"Well, Stash, why were you walking in the first place? Did you not have your own vehicle?"

"No, Mr. John. I didn't own a vehicle at that time. The only way I had of going anywhere was on my motorcycle. I would ride it over to his house and then rode from there to work with him in his car."

"Stash, which motorcycle was that? Was it the XL 100 or the 550 Suzuki? Now which one did you say you ended up in the ditch with that morning you said your lunch box failed from between your legs?"

"Now, Mr. John, you didn't need to go and bring that back up. That was over thirty years ago when that took place. You know now that I think back to the day in which I walked off the job. It was that very morning that I ended up in the ditch with the 550 Suzuki on my back. Thanks, Mr. John, for reminding me of that unforgettable day. Now just what time is it getting to be?"

"Why do you ask? What's on your mind, Stash?"

"Why do you keep calling me Stash, Mr. John?"

"Well, it just seems to fit you."

"Whatever you say, John, but I don't think I like it."

"Well, Stash, that beautiful young lady sure likes calling you by that name."

"John, it's okay for her alone to call me that, but I don't understand why she is calling me by that name. I guess when I go see her tomorrow, I'll find out. I'm going to say goodnight."

I went to my room and read in the book of Psalm 24, and as I read this, I came to these verses which said:

> He shall receive the blessing from the Lord, and righteousness from the God of his salvation. This is the generation of them that seek him, that seek thy face, O Jacob. Selah. As I continue to read on down in to. (Ps. 24:25–26)
>
> Unto thee, O Lord, do I lift up my soul. O my God, I trust in thee: let me not be ashamed, let not mine enemies triumph over me… Shew me thy ways, O Lord; teach me thy paths. Lead me in thy truth, and teach me: for thou art the God of my salvation; on thee do I wait all the day. (Ps. 25:1–2, 4–5)

Good night, and may God be your guardian, protector, and teacher in all your days.

* * * * *

"Good morning, Mrs. John. Where is your grumpy old man at this morning?"

"Oh, good morning to you also, Mr. Stash. John went over to check on the work being done to the house. He said to tell you not to forget to go see Ms. Sue down at the coffee shop this morning."

"No, ma'am. I hadn't forgotten. I was going to go and see her after stopping by the dock and speaking with the captain to see how the work is coming with the ship. Mrs. John, do you know if Mr. John has internet here?"

"No, I'm not sure if we have internet, Stash. Why do you ask?"

"I'm just curious to see if I can connect to my e-mail and see if my first book has come out or not. I will check down at the coffee shop and see if they have Wi-Fi there. I see you later, Mrs. John." As I made my way to the dock, I remembered a time when my brother and I was out playing with my cousins and we came across some blueberries. They decided to crush them all over my back, making it look as if I had fell on a sharp object, injuring myself. Our grandma was up for a visit. They carried me to the house and called her. She came out and saw my back covered with the blueberry stain. She became upset because she thought I had seriously got injured. She asked, "What in the world has happened to him?" They began to laugh, but she didn't see the humor in what they had done. She sent us to get a gall berry limb. Do I need to say what came next?

Now I would look back on those good old days. I would remember going down to her house; she lived in the community of Good Hope, which is in Perry County. As young boys, we would go spend time with her. We would walk about three miles to this store. Back in those days, they would put little men with parachutes in with the bubblegum. Back then, you could get a pack of gum for five cents. When we got back from the store, we would climb her sycamore trees she had in the front yard, threw the little men out, and watched them float to the ground. Oh, how I missed those days as a young boy doing little things such as that.

"Good morning, Captain. How is everything coming with the work?"

"Oh, Stash."

"Oh, wait just a minute, Captain. Why are you now calling me Stash?"

"Well, son, I have heard that is your new name that Ms. Sue has given you."

"Okay, Captain. You know that is not my name. Now once again, how is the work coming?"

"It's coming along a lot better now that we have the engineers working alongside us. I just wish we could move a little faster than what we are. I need to get back out on the ocean. I'm not making any money sitting here on land. I know you are also wanting to get out of this desert. What do you say we go on down to the coffee shop for breakfast, Son?"

"Sir, that is the best idea I've heard all morning. I was planning on going by to see Ms. Sue after I had talked with you. She had left word for me to come by. She wanted to talk with me about something."

As we made our way to the coffee shop, we'd talk about how we could speed up the work around the ship. We made it to the coffee shop only to find that Ms. Sue had to take off this morning to keep her meeting with her divorce lawyer.

"Ma'am, do you know if she is coming in at all today?"

"Stash, she left this note for you."

"Oh, she left a note for me."

"Stash, what does she say in her note?"

"It says right here on the front, 'For your eyes only, Stash.' Now, Captain, that tells me that she is wanting me to keep it to myself."

"Well, okay then, keep it to yourself. I didn't really want to know anyway. But you just remember this, it's my ship that you need to get out of this desert that you have found yourself to be in."

"Well, Captain, for your information, your ship is not the only one that comes here carrying supplies. Ma'am do you have Wi-Fi here in the store? I would like to check my email and see if there is any update when my book is to be coming out."

"Yes, Stash, we do. But you will need the password to logon with. Here, you can use my computer if you would like. I don't mind if you use it."

"Thank you, Marianne. That is very nice of you. I go to my website, and there it appears both hardcover, paperback, and e-book. Oh, wow. Now what is this?"

"What is what, Stash"?

"Marianne, look at this short video that Christian Faith Publishing Company did about my first book. Marianne, they sure have gone all out on promoting this little book that I wrote. I wonder if anyone has made any comments about it. Look, I got a message from Keith Brewer."

"Stash, just who is this person?"

"Marianne, he's one of my friends that I graduated with from Clara High School, back in the good old days. I wonder what he's been up to these days."

"What does he have to say? Is it anything about your book?"

"I don't know. I haven't open it yet."

"What are you waiting on, Stash? I would like to know what he has to say."

"Marianne, now if you don't mind, just give me a minute, okay?"

"'Son, I am sorry for not getting back with you about reading this amazing book. I caught myself wanting to get to the next chapter. You are truly an amazing person with a gift—it's called faith. If I ever need someone to have my back, it is you. I have my life's soul mate and blessed with two amazing children. As I am reading your book, it really hit home of just how blessed I am. Thank you, sir, my friend.' Here, Marianne, you can read it for yourself.

"I never thought that I could write anything that could have an impact on someone's life such as this. Mom has always said that your name would go further than your face ever would go in life. Thank you, Marianne, for the use of your computer. I am going to head back to the shop and tell Mr. and Mrs. John that my first book has come out: Oh, by the way, please tell Sue I will come back to see her later today."

As I was making my way back to Mr. and Mrs. John's, I started thinking about starting a new book. But what could this one be about? I could write a story maybe about an American soldier, but there was just one thing—what would this story be about? Oh, wait just a minute. I could tell the story about myself as an American soldier and name it, *The Footprints of an American Soldier* or *The Footsteps of an American Soldier*. I thought it would be a great story to write about, but just when would I find the time to write such a story?

"Good afternoon, Mr. John. How are you?"

"Oh, Stash, I'm doing okay, just hot. Did you happen to stop by the coffee shop to see your friend?"

"Yes, I did. Why do you ask?"

"Well, she came by earlier today to see you."

"Did she say what she wanted to see me about?"

"She didn't say. She just said that she needed to see you."

"Marianne said she was not there. She had to take off to go see her lawyer. You know, she's in the process of getting a divorce. She caught her husband with another woman under a bridge three months ago. I have heard that they are now calling it the River Bridge Motel. They say that you can check in at no cost. That's if you are willing to take the risk of getting caught by your significant other.

I'm going back later this afternoon to see her.

"I got some good news while I was there. Marianne let me use her computer to check on my first book, and it is now out on Amazon and Barnes & Nobles. They also did a short video about it. I also got a message from a friend whom I graduated high school with. He said that he was very impressed with the book. He also gave me a new idea on how to promote it. He said that it looked like a floor mat, as for the cover goes."

"That is great, Stash. I would like to read it for myself to see just how great of a job you did on writing it. I would also like to see if I can find the different chapters in the book which you said that you took these parts from and came up with these chapters."

"On my way here, Mr. John, I was thinking of writing a book about a soldier. What do you think, sir?"

"Stash, do you think that would be a good story to write about?"

"John, I don't see why I couldn't do it. After all, I do have somewhat the ability to use my imagination on telling stories."

"Stash, if you need any help, Mrs. John would be more than happy to help you in correcting your grammar and putting your sentences in proper order when needed."

"Do you really think she would, Mr. John?"

"Yes, Stash. I do believe she would love to help you in telling your story about a soldier who is proud to serve his country that he loves. When do you think you will start on it, and just who will this soldier be?"

"Mr. John, the story will be about myself."

"Do what? It be will about yourself?"

"Yes, sir. I do have two older brothers—one joined the air force, and the oldest joined the Mississippi National Guard. I have always looked to my oldest brother as being a father figure for he became the man of the house at a young age of nine after our father had passed away. I learned a lot from him as we are growing up back in the day. He was the one who convinced me to join the military after high school and use the GI Bill to get a higher degree, but I didn't use it for myself. I decided to pass it to my two children for them to use.

"I'm going to head back down to the coffee shop to see if Ms. Sue has gotten back from her visit with her lawyer and tell her about my book. Just maybe she will be as happy to hear that it is now out, but I don't know. She may not be in a good mood after meeting with her lawyer today—I know. I wasn't all that happy after meeting with my lawyer during the time of my divorce. She did say she would love to read it once it has come out."

"Stash, before you go see your lovely lady and tell her all about your book, could you tell me some more of your childhood stories?"

"Well, I guess one would be okay. I was still working night shift, operating the package maker. My oldest brother was operating the striper. This one particular night, the trim saw got out of time with the solar and was mixing up lumber by grade and length. It was my job to separate the mixed lumber. My brother came up to my workstation and started saying words I never heard before. I told him he was not going to talk to me in that manner. I was just doing my job. If he didn't like it, he could find himself another ride home that night. At the end of our shift, I went out and got in my truck, leaving him. It took all I could to leave him that night. He was the one who got me the job working at the sawmill back in January 1985.

"Now there are more stories I could tell you, but I need to go see if Ms. Sue is back. I'll see you later."

As I made my way to see Ms. Sue, I remembered this one afternoon in April. Our supervisor was on vacation; he had someone else filling in for him. Well, it started to snow, making roads hazardous to travel. We left work before the roads became hard to travel. We had a friend to ask if we could follow her home to see that she made it home okay. We went a different way than what we would normally travel. I was behind them. We came up to the end of the road which had a hill, and you then had to go right or left. They made it with no problem, but it didn't go that well for me. It took me three or four times to get up the hill in my truck. My brother was at the top of the hill waiting on me. He asked, "What took you so long?"

"Man, I was slipping and sliding all over the hill. I was beginning to think that I was not going to make it up the hill. I began to think that you were going to have to pull me up from it," I answered.

"That's all the time I have, John. I do need to be going.

"Good afternoon, Ms. Sue. How's your day going?"

"Stash, it's going okay, but not as great as I would like for it to be. My lawyer said that my soon- to-be ex-husband is being stubborn about giving me the divorce that I have asked for. He's now saying that he does not want to give me a divorce because he feels that he didn't do anything wrong by being caught with another woman under a bridge. I'm like, 'Really? I got pictures of them both.' Now, Stash, I ask of you, does that not sound just like a man who's cheating on his wife, who has been by his side through thick and thin for over twenty years and is the mother of his children? I will never understand, Stash, how some people can cheat on their spouse and think that they have never done anything wrong. I would never in my life do anything like that to him. But now that he has done this to me, I can't see myself living with him any longer. Just how could someone do that and live with themselves, Stash?"

"Sue, that is a question I have asked myself for the past two years, and to this day, I have no answer. Now may I ask you a question?"

"Sure, Stash. What's on your mind?"

"Sue, I would like to know why you are calling me Stash."

"Well, I love a man with a mustache. It makes him look very intelligent. I hope you aren't offended in anyway by me calling you Stash."

"Oh no, ma'am. I'm not at all offended. Now if you don't mind me asking, just what is your lawyer advising you to do next?"

"He said that I can go ahead with the divorce procedures since I got the pictures to prove that the two of them have been meeting secretly. He feels that the judge would have no problem in granting me my divorce from him."

"Sue, I do hope the very best for you and your children, for no one should have to go through what you and your children are going through. People just don't stop and think about their actions and the outcome it has on everyone involved. They only seem to be thinking of themselves at the time they are committing such an act. No offense intended here, Ms. Sue, but may we change the subject now?"

"Sure, what would you like to talk about, Stash?"

"Well, how about my first book? It is now out on Amazon, Barnes & Noble, and it's also available as an e-book."

"Stash, that is great news. I'm so proud to hear that. I hope it does great for you."

"So do I, Sue. I did get a great review from one of my friends whom I graduated high school with, and one from my coworker who said he was looking forward to reading the sequel when it comes out."

"That's great news, Stash. I'm glad to hear some good news for a change, even if it is only about your little book that you wrote about you being on a journey, looking all over the world for a soulmate. I'm looking forward to reading it."

"So, Sue, I take it you're impressed about my first book being out. I was thinking about doing a third book. I'm sure it would be interesting to write about one's life in the military."

"Oh yes. Now Stash, that sounds like a great idea. When will you get started on it?"

"Well, Ms. Sue, I have some stories that I could write about. One being my life as a soldier serving his country which I'm proud to be a part of."

"Stash, I didn't know you were a soldier."

"Yes, ma'am. I thought about joining the marines back before graduating high school, but I decided to follow in my oldest brother's footsteps and joined the Mississippi National Guard after graduating."

"Wow, Stash, I would love to hear some of your stories about you serving in the military and the places you have been."

"Ms. Sue, there are more stories about my childhood I would like to write about before I go into writing about my life as a soldier, one being the time when my sister and I came home from school. We had gotten into an argument on the bus about something. We went into the house, I put my books down on the bar, and the next thing I knew, she had hit me in the back of the head with her fist. It was as if she had hit me with one of Mom's cast-iron skillet."

"Did it hurt?"

"Yes, it hurt. I saw stars for about thirty seconds."

Are you sure it was her fist and not one of your mom's skillet?"

"Yes, I'm sure it was her fist because later, she said her fist was hurting. Now that I think back on those days, my oldest brother and I got into it on the bus about me having the window down. He wanted me to let it up. I didn't want to let it up. He told me that he was going to get me when we got off the bus. When we did get off the bus, he started chasing me. I ran around the pump house to get away from him. He came in full speed after me around the pump house. As he did, his feet went out from under him, giving me time to get away. As I look back on them old days, I can only say they were some of the best days of my life.

"Ms. Sue, talking with you has been nice. I am going to say goodnight now. May God watch over you until we meet again."

"Same to you, Stash. Be safe on your way home tonight. Oh, wait, Stash. Would you like to have dinner with me tonight? I would like to hear more about your time growing up in the small community of Mulberry."

"Now, Ms. Sue, I don't think that would be a good idea because you are still married, and you know how some people like to spread gossip."

"Stash, if you would like, we can have dinner here with Marianne. No one would say anything."

"Well, Sue, if you feel it'll be okay, and if Marianne would be willing to stay and have dinner with us, I guess it'd be okay just this once."

"Good, I'll go ask her. I'll be right back." Sue then said, "She said that it would be nice."

"Okay, Sue, I'll see you both back here around seven. I need to head down to the dock to meet with the captain on how the work is coming on getting the ship back out on the ocean."

* * * * *

"Good afternoon, Captain. How is everything coming on getting the ship back out to the ocean?"

"Stash, I got some good news. It looks like we'll be back out to sea in about two to three days, that's if everything goes as planned."

As he was telling me this, I was thinking, "Boy, I'm so glad to hear this news."

"Oh, Stash, are you still planning on going with us?"

"Yes, sir. I do plan on leaving this desert with you, that's if you don't mind."

"No, Stash, I don't mind at all."

"Okay, Captain, I'll check back with you tomorrow. I'm going to tell Mr. John the good news."

* * * * *

"Good afternoon, Mr. and Mrs. John. I got some great news today. The captain said that if everything goes as he hopes, we will be able to set sail in about two or three days."

"Son, that is great. Are you planning to leave even with everything you have going on here with Ms. Sue? I'm also hoping you would stay and let Mrs. John help you with your new book that you were planning on writing."

"What do you mean 'everything,' Mr. John? I don't have anything going on with Ms. Sue. Besides, she is still married, and we don't know when her divorce will be final. I don't have anything going on with anyone else here in this desert place. I do plan on having dinner tonight with her and Marianne at the coffee shop. I'm going to tell her that I'm planning on leaving with the captain when he leaves. As for me writing my next book, I guess I can write it while I'm out on the ocean."

"Well, son, I'm going to miss having you around. Hearing you tell about yourself as you were growing up makes my day. I'm just sorry that the lady you came here with took off with some other guy."

"Mr. John, so am I. But now that you have mentioned her, there is something I need to go do."

"Son, may I ask just what would that be?"

"I would like to give her one more chance. Do you remember when I told you about the one solid yellow and red rose, and me wanting to write her one more note explaining the way I felt for her luscious love? Mr. John, only if she had let me have the key to her fragile heart, I feel that we could have made a great helpmate for each other. But she felt that she needed to go in a different direction without even giving me a second look. John, can I borrow one of your motorcycles tomorrow to go into the next town and see if I can find one solid yellow and red rose?"

"Son, you know I don't mind you using one. I just thought about something, son. Why don't you invite Marianne and Sue over here for dinner, and you can tell us all some more stories about yourself?"

"Mr. John, that is a great idea. Do you think Mrs. John be okay with it?

"Son, you know she will. She would love to have them over for dinner. You can entertain us with your crazy stories."

"Okay, Mr. John. I will go and let them know that we will be having dinner with you and Mrs. John tonight."

On my way to let Marianne and Sue know that we'll be having dinner with Mr. John, I began to remember a time when my youngest brother and I went to one of our friend's father's funeral. We were riding our motorcycles. When we left the funeral, I noticed that my chain was making a noise. I didn't think much about it at the time, so we got on the highway, and he opened the one he was on up. I tried to keep up with him, but the chain just got louder. I slowed down until I could find a place to pull over and tighten the chain up, but to my surprise, it was not just the chain being loose, the teeth on the front sprocket was almost gone. So I had to ease my way home that afternoon. The person I bought it from wanted to trade me a pickup for the bike. I told him before we traded that it needed a front sprocket and some other work done to it. He said that he wanted the bike anyway, so we traded.

I then remembered riding that bike over to our friend's house and helping them haul pulpwood. We had to load the wood on the truck by hand back in those days. As I looked back on those days, I could say they were some of the best days of my life as a teenager working for money to buy the things I needed for school. The only way you got what you wanted was to work for it, just like your parents had to work to put food on the table for you, clothes on your back, and shoes on your feet.

Children nowadays have no clue what those days were like, having to work for what you needed. All they know nowadays is how to play games on their cell phones and computers. It appears that they don't know how to work for the extra things that they want. They expect you to just hand everything to them without them even working for it.

DINNER AT MR. AND MRS. JOHN WITH SUE AND MARIANNE

"**H**ELLO, DARLING. I CAME BACK to let you and Marianne know that Mr. John has invited us to their place for dinner tonight. That's if you would like to."

"Stash, that's very nice of him to invite us over for dinner. I'm sure we'll enjoy ourselves. What time do we need to be there? Do we need to bring anything?"

"Sue, he didn't say. But if you would like, you can bring one of your favorite pie. Oh, before I for-

get, Sue, I got some good news from the captain today."

"What good news would that be, Stash?" He told me that the ship would be able to set sail within two or three days if everything continues to go as planned."

"Stash, that is good news. Are you still planning on going with them?"

"I'm not sure, Sue. There's something that I need to do before I leave here."

"What would that be, Stash, if you don't mind me asking?"

"Sue, I don't mind you asking, but I'm not going to say right now. I'll be back to pick you and Marianne up around six."

"Okay, Stash, we'll see you then."

As I headed back to Mr. John's, I took a long walk down by the ocean. As I walked, I began to reflect on some of my fondest memories when I first joined the 624th Quartermaster Company in Waynesboro, Mississippi. Before talking about those days, I remembered my oldest brother sending me and my youngest brother a pair of combat boots from Fort Leopardwood. He told us not to wear them until he came home from his basic training for he wanted to show us how to spit-shine them before we could wear them. When he got home that summer, he showed us how to put a shine on them where you could see your reflection. I decided to wear mine to school one day. I had a teacher that year who was also in the military. He began to tell me how I could really make my boots shine. So when I got home that day from school, I tried what he had told me. By the time I was done with both boots, my index finger was as black as they were, but I got to say they did shine like a mirror. My brother said from that day on, if I wanted to continue to wear them to school, I had to keep them looking that good.

"Good afternoon, Mrs. John. Do you know where Mr. John is?"

"No, I don't know. If he's not somewhere out in the shop, son, I have no idea where he could be. Did he tell you that Ms. Sue and Ms. Marianne are coming over for dinner tonight?"

"Yes, son, he told me that he asked you to invite them over tonight."

"I told them I would be back to pick them up at six. If that's okay with you, Mrs. John."

"Son, I don't mind at all. What would you like me to fix for dinner?"

"Ma'am, whatever you fix will be fine with me. I'm going to see if I can find John somewhere in the shop."

"Son, when you find him, tell him I need for you two to go pick up some greens and beans, lamb chops, salt, flour, tea, and anything else that he can think of for dinner."

"Ma'am, will you please write that down for me? That's a lot to remember."

"Okay, son, I'll write it down."

* * * * *

"Oh, John, your wife has asked for us to go to the grocery store and pick up these things for dinner tonight. John, I've been doing some thinking over the past few hours about leaving on the ship in the next three days."

"Son, I know you are all excited about getting out of this desert that you have found yourself to be in, but can I give you some advice?"

"What would that advice be, Mr. John?"

"Son, you know at one time in my life, I found myself to be where you are. You know when my wife passed away, I felt that I needed to get married again. So I started dating any woman that would have anything to do with me. I went all over this ole world looking for someone to replace the one true love I had lost, but I came to realize later that dating just any woman was not the right thing for me or my two sons. So I decided to stop looking for that one true love until the day Ms. Mary came back into my life. I got to say she has given my life a whole new meaning. Son, you are a young man. Therefore, there is no need for you to go rushing into a relationship with any woman that you are not interested in. Now, son, you have all the time in the world to find the right woman who holds the same kind of love in her heart for you as you have for her. Son, I'm not trying to tell you what to do in anyway here. After all, you are very capable of making up your own mind. I just want you to know, son, that you are more than welcome to stay at the shop if you want."

"Mr. John, that is very nice of you to make such an offer to me. You and Mary have gone out of your way to make my stay here a very pleasant one. I don't know what else I can say other than thank you both. John, look what time it has gotten to be. We need to get these things back to the house or Mrs. John won't have time to cook them for dinner. Besides, I got to go pick up Sue and Marianne."

* * * * *

"Mrs. Mary, here are the things you asked for, and Mr. John did pick up some other things he say he would love for you to cook tonight for the ladies. Is there anything that I can do to help you before I go pick them up?"

"No, son, there's nothing at this time that I can think of. Besides, you need to head out to pick them up. It is almost six. I'll have everything done by the time you'll get back. Will you tell John I would like to see him on your way out?"

"Yes, ma'am. I'll tell him on my way out if I see him."

* * * * *

"Mr. John, Ms. Mary would like to see you in the kitchen."
"Okay, thanks, son."

* * * * *

"Yes, ma'am, what do you need?"
"Oh, John, just come in here, please."
"Yes, ma'am. What can I do for you, my love?"
"We need to talk about all this food that you want me to cook."
"Ma'am, you know I like to go all out for our friends and family."
"Well, John, I hope that our friends and family has a big appetite with all this food you have asked me to prepare. Now will you please go set the table for me?"
"Yes, ma'am. Do you think that we can get Son to talk about some of his experience of being in the military tonight over dinner?"
"John, I don't know. We can ask him if he would like to talk about those days."

* * * * *

"Hello, Ms. Sue, are you and Marianne ready to have dinner with Mr. and Mrs. John?"

"Stash, we have been looking forward to this dinner ever since you told us that they had invited us over tonight. Now give us about five minutes and we will be ready."

"Okay, Sue, I'll just have a cup of coffee while I wait."

"Stash, we are ready to go."

"Sue, you know while on my way over here, I started thinking about something."

"Oh no, Stash, you haven't been thinking again now, have you?"

"Ha-ha, very funny, ladies. Just for that, I'm not going to share my thoughts with you."

"Now, Stash, you know we were just joking with you. Now come on, tell us just what were you thinking about."

"Well, okay, I was thinking, if a woman was to have an abortion, would that not be committing murder of her unborn child?"

"Stash, I'll never understand how some people can say that it's not committing murder. And I sometimes wonder what this world would be like if the ones who believe that abortion is not murder, what would they be saying to their mother if she was thinking of having abortion while she was still pregnant them?"

"Marianne, what do you think they would say to their mother if she was considering of having abortion while she was still pregnant with them?"

"Well, Stash, I don't know how to answer that question because I too can't even come close of understanding the way they think. I see murder as being just what it is, murder. The only way I can see taking the life of an unborn child is if the mother's life is in imminent danger of losing her own life, and for someone taking the life of another person would be in self-defense of their own life or the life of a loved one."

"Well, ladies, I am thinking their unborn child would be telling their mother not to have abortion because they one day might grow up to become a doctor, a lawyer, or maybe a judge, or even a king of some country. But I'm guessing, ladies, this is something we will never know because their mothers apparently thought that having abortion would be committing murder of her unborn child."

"Stash, can I ask you something?"

"Sure, Sue, what's on your mind?"

"Did you feel the presence of the Lord thy God around you? Because I did the whole time we were talking about this subject."

"Yes, ma'am. I did. And by you asking me this reminds me of a time when I was on my way home from work one day. I came up on this person who looked to be in need of help, so I stopped and asked if he needed help. He replied, 'Yes, can you please give me a ride to the hospital? I had been jumped by some other person who got the best of me.'"

"Stash, did you give him a ride to the hospital after he told you that he had been in a fight?"

"Yes, I did because when I saw him in need of someone's help, I was reminded of this story in the Bible."

Which story is that, Stash?"

"You both know the parable of the Good Samaritan that Jesus spoke of in the book of Luke. It's about a person who was stripped of clothing, then beaten and left half dead alongside the road. First, a priest and then a Levite came by, but both avoided the man. But a certain Samaritan, as he journeyed, came where he was. And when he saw him, he had compassion on him. And went to him, and bound up his wounds, pouring in oil and wine, and set him on his own beast, and brought him to an inn, and took care of him. It's found in Luke 10:30–34.

"Now you ladies both know Jesus said that where two or three are gathered in his name, he is there with them."

"Yes, Stash, you are right. And you know also in 1 Thessalonians 5:16, it says, "Rejoice evermore. Pray without ceasing. In everything, give thanks, for this is the will of God in Christ Jesus concerning you. Quench not the Spirit." Knowing this, I just can't help but to praise his holy name for every blessing he has blessed me with. Thank you, Lord. Thank you for loving me for who I am."

"Ladies, that reminds me there is something I need to look up in the Bible."

"What would that be, Stash?"

I'm thinking there's some passages where God says he will put in every heart of mankind a merge of his love for every person will know him."

"Why do you need to look that up, Stash?"

"Well, I would like to know for sure if I'm saying it just the way it is said in the Bible. I don't like to tell someone something and not know what I'm talking about. For I have read in the book of Ephesians 4:15, it says, 'But speaking the truth in love, may grow up into him in all things, which is the head, even Christ.'

"I know there are some people who already look at me as if I don't know what I'm talking about. Just look at what you said to me when I told you that I had done some thinking on my way over to pick you two up for dinner."

"Yes, Stash, but did I not also tell you I was joking with you?"

"Yes, Sue, you did. Now let's go in for dinner. Mrs. John has been preparing a great meal for us tonight."

"Stash, you never did tell us what she was cooking tonight."

"Sue, I know she is cooking turnip green, butterbeans and lamb chops, some cornbread, and other things that Mr. John picked up from the grocery store."

"Has she cooked all of that just for us tonight for dinner? Well, Stash, I don't know if I can eat that much food. How about you, Marianne?"

"Oh, I came with a hearty appetite. I'm sure I can eat my share."

* * * * *

"Good evening, Mr. and Mrs. John. How are you two?"

"Well, hello, young ladies. It's nice to have you over for dinner. I hope you came with a big appetite."

"Yes, ma'am. From what Stash had told us that you have prepared for us, if we leave hungry, it'll be our own fault."

"Yes, child. He is right there. John has asked me to prepare a meal to feed an army."

"Now, ma'am, you know I have also asked my two sons and their wives to join us tonight. I need to call them and see where they are. They should have been here by now."

"Did you tell them what time to be here?"

"Yes, I told them to be here at seven."

"John, I just heard someone pulled up. It might be them."

"Hey, come on in. I was about to call you two. Mary is ready to eat."

"John, are you going to introduce our guest?"

"Oh, right. Ms. Sue, Marianne, meet Jim and his wife Jammie, and Mork and his wife Mendy. And y'all know Stash already."

"Okay, John. Now will you give thanks? I'm ready to eat."

"Yes, ma'am. Lord, we give thanks unto you for our friends and families who have gathered here tonight, for the good health in which you have so blessed us with. Oh, Lord, it's by your hands alone that we can partake of this food that provides our body with the needed nutrients to maintain our health. Amen.

"Let's eat. Now, Stash, are you going to tell us some more of your childhood stories?"

Oh yes. Will you please, please, Stash? I would love to hear some of your stories when you were growing up back in the late sixties and mid-eighties."

"Well, if you insist. There might be one or two that I can recall. My oldest brother and I took a trip one day down what we call memory lane. This memory lane took us back in time to a place long ago where I just remember some small parts of it. I was about three or four at the time, he said. Our family went down to visit Mom's second cousin who owned some horses, cows, and goats. We would sometimes ride the horses if we were not playing other games. Well, it came time for us to head back home because they had to go somewhere, but their car would not start, so dad offered to jump their vehicle off. When they hooked the jumper cables to each vehicle's batteries and he went to start the car, the battery blew up, so dad had to take him to get a new battery.

"While we were waiting for them to get back from town, his wife told us a story about a time when he had to get up in the middle of the night to go to the outhouse, and the door locked behind him.

She went on to say that he was running around the house, hollering at the top of his lungs, opening the door, 'There's this crazy billy goat after me. Will someone please open the door? This crazy billy goat is trying to ram me.'"

"Did anyone ever get up and open the door for him?"

"She said after his third time around the house, screaming at the top of his lungs, she got up and let him back in. Now this story about a locked door reminds me of another story that I will share with you later. While I'm on this memory lane, I remember a time when Mom took us children to register for preschool. My youngest sister crawled across the seat and accidentally pulled the gear shifter into neutral, letting the car roll back across the road, ending up in the ditch. Mom came running to the car to see if we were all right. After seeing we were all right, she tore my backside up for letting her do such a thing.

"Man, look at the time. It has gotten late, and I need to get you ladies back."

"Yes, son."

"We do need to be getting on back. We open the store in the morning. Mrs. John, thank you for dinner tonight. We have enjoyed it. It was nice to have met you all. Hope we can get together some other time."

"Marianne, Sue, it was also nice to have met you, and yes, maybe one day soon we can get together for another night out."

"Mr. John before I take these ladies back home, can you tell me where in the Bible that God says that he will put a measure of his Spirit in every mankind's heart?"

"Son, I'm not sure if I know there's a scripture in the Bible where it says that in the way you said, but I do recall in the book of Ezekiel 36: 26, it talks about God giving man a new heart."

"Okay, thanks, Mr. John. I will look it up when I get back from taking these ladies home. Ladies, are you ready to head home?"

"Yes, we are ready, Stash.:

"Well, ladies, we have once again made it back safe. Thank you, Marianne, for having dinner with us. Good night to you both."

"Stash, wait. I would like to talk with you if you don't mind."

"Sure, what's on your mind, Marianne?"

"Oh wait just a minute now Marianne, you need stop doing that. You are a married woman, and you know I don't get involved in a romantic act with a married woman. After being married for twenty-five years, I have come to know what true love really means to me and to share that kind of love with someone without knowing within my own heart would be committing a sin. Marianne, that is the very reason why I asked Sue to ask you to join us tonight for dinner at Mrs. John's, simply because I didn't want to be seen out with just one married woman."

"Oh now, Stash, I'm not married. I'm single as one woman can be."

"Then why do you wear a wedding band?"

"I wear them because there are men out there who like hitting on me, and I don't like them doing that. Now the wedding band that you see on my finger was given to me by my mother. She told me when she gave them to me that they once belonged to my grandmother. She asked her to give them to me on my twenty-first birthday, even if I was married by then or not. Now do you still want me to stop?"

"Marianne, you are a very attractive woman, who any man would be proud to have you as his wife. Now at one time in my life when I was a much younger man and before I got married, I would have said, 'No, don't stop.' Marianne, even though I'm very tempted with your offer, I'm not going to say yes, simply because I don't want us to end up doing something that we both would be sorry for later. And besides, Marianne, we hardly know one other."

"Stash, you can't blame a girl for trying now, can you?"

"No, Marianne, I can't at all blame you. You are a very beautiful woman. And if I knew beyond a shadow of a doubt in my heart that I could tell you that I love you, I would, before you could blink an eye. But I can't, and mean it in the way you deserve to hear it."

"Stash, I must say your honesty is just one of the unique things I do find very attractive about you. You are a man who is very faithful to your beliefs, for there are men in this world today who would not stick to their beliefs like you do. It appears men of this world today would love to jump in to bed with a woman at the first chance they get, regardless if they both are married or not. And I'm not saying married to each other. Do you know what I'm saying, Stash?"

"Yes, I do know just what you are saying, but may I add that it isn't just men. It's also women who are inviting the other men into their homes. Now thank you, Marianne, for the very kind words you said earlier. I must be going now. Once again, goodnight, and may God keep his loving hands around you until we met again."

"Okay, Stash. Good night to you also, and once again, thank you, Mrs. John, for dinner tonight. I did enjoy myself."

"Yes, ma'am. I'll be sure to let her know when I get back."

* * * * *

"Mrs. John, the ladies asked me to tell you they enjoyed the dinner you cooked for them. Mr. John, Mrs. John, I also want to say a big thanks to you both for the lovely dinner. You both went way beyond what you should have."

"Oh, son, it was our pleasure to have you all here tonight. Son, before you head off to bed, could you tell us one more story of your trip down memory lane with your brother?"

"Well, okay. I guess I can share one with you before I go to bed. Now after leaving the story about the billy goat, we talked about when I first started school at Glade. Glade school was where I got into my first fight ever."

"What did you get into a fight about?"

"We were out playing, and one of the other boys pushed me down. I got up and pushed him back. He then in return hit me in the nose, causing it to bleed. One of the teachers went and got the school nurse. She put a pair of cold scissors to the back of my neck. She told me that would stop the bleeding."

"Son, by her putting cold scissors to the back of your neck, did it stop the bleeding?"

"Yes, ma'am. The bleeding did finally stop after a few minutes. Ma'am, I'm going to say good night now. Mr. John, what book did you say you thought God says he will give man a new heart?"

"Son, it is in the book of Ezekiel 36:26, and you also might want to look in Romans 12:3."

"Okay, thanks, John. I will take a look at them both before I go to bed."

* * * * *

As I read in the book of Ezekiel chapter 36 starting with verse 22 through 27, it had this to say:

> Therefore, say unto the house of Israel, Thus, saith the Lord God; I do not this for your sakes, O house of Israel, but for mine holy name's sake, which ye have profaned among the heathen, whither ye went. And I will sanctify my great name, which was profaned among the heathen, which ye have profaned in the midst of them; and the heathen shall know that I am the Lord, saith the Lord God, when I shall be sanctified in you before their eyes. For I will take you from among the heathen, and gather you out of all countries, and will bring you into your own land. Then will I sprinkle clean water upon you, and ye shall be clean: from all your filthiness, and from all your idols, will I cleanse you. A new heart also will I give you, and a new spirit will I put within you: and I will take away the stony heart out of your flesh, and I will give you an heart of flesh. And I will put my spirit with-in you, and cause you to walk in my statutes, and ye shall keep my judgments, and do them. (Ezek. 36:22–27)

Now let's look also in the book of Romans 12:3 and see what it had to say:

> For I say, through the grace given unto me, to every man that isamong you, not to think of him-self more highly than he ought tothink; but to think

soberly, according as God hath dealt to every man the measure of faith.

After reading these scriptures, I'm going to say goodnight. Thank you for sharing your valuable time with me today, friend. May God bless you all with his love forevermore.

* * * * *

"Good morning, Mrs. John. How are you?"

"Oh, good morning, Son I'm doing great for God has blessed me with another day. How about yourself?"

"Oh, you are right about that, Mrs. John. God has really blessed us with another beautiful day."

"Son, if you don't mind me asking, what's your plan for today?"

"Well, I was planning on going over to Seaport town at some point today and see if I can find a single yellow and red rose."

"Son, why are you still stuck on trying to impress Ms. Jimi? Don't you know that she couldn't care less about you?"

"Yes, ma'am. I know that just by the way she took off with you-know-who, and I'm okay with that because I know she is a grown woman and she has every right to share her love with whomever she so chooses. It's not in any way that I'm trying to impress her because I know within my own heart you can't make someone love you like you love them. But before I do move on with the next part of my life journey, I would like to show her my gratitude for saving my life that day out there in the desert. If it had not been for her, I may not be here today."

"Son, you are a very kindhearted person for wanting to show her your gratitude, but I got to ask, do you think she will be half as grateful as you are?"

"Mrs. John, I can't answer that kind of question because I don't know her heart, and sometimes, I don't feel as if I know my own. Now with the way this conversation seems to be going, I'm going to need another big cup of your coffee.

"Good morning, Mr. John. How are you?"

"I'm okay, thanks for asking."

Mom, will you please fix me your famous French toast with scrambled eggs and butter grits?"

"John, will there be anything else that I can fix for you?"

"No, ma'am. That be all for now. Oh, wait, my sweet honeybun. I'll have a cup of coffee as well.

"Now, son, are you still planning on going to Seaport today?"

"Yes, sir, I am. That's if you are still going to let me use one of your vehicles."

"Son, you know I don't mind you using one, but I'm going to go with you."

"Now, John, just what reason do you have for going with him?"

"Mom, there are some parts I need to pick up for one of the bikes I'm working on."

"John, that is great. Now I can take the truck and trackhoe back now that the engineers are done with it. What time do you want leave?"

"Son, as so as I can find the invoice, we can go."

"Well, John, while you are looking for the invoice, I'm going to head on down to the dock and see if they have the trackhoe loaded."

"Now hold on, son, it won't take me but just a minute to get the invoice. It's on the end table by my recliner."

"Here, John, is this the one?"

"Yes, sweetie. That is the one, thank you."

"Son, did you remember to get the money for the payment on the trackhoe?"

"Yes, sir. Got it right here. Oh, wait, this is not the money. It's a note I was working on last night."

"Son, have you been trying to write again?"

"Just you never mind, John, about my writing. The money was in my other pocket. Now can we be on our way?"

"Son, I hope you are not mad for what I said earlier. I was just kidding with you about your writing."

"No, John, you didn't because I know there are people who really don't like what I have said in my writing."

"Well, son, I'm sorry you feel that way because you know Mrs. John, Sue, and the captain have said they like what you have written this far in your journey."

"Yes, sir. I know that. But they are just three people out of who knows how many other who don't like it."

"Son, you need not to worry about the people who don't like it. Just be happy for the ones who do."

"I guess you are right."

"Son, you know I'm right. Now can I read the note you are working on?"

"No, you can't because it's going to be for Ms. Jimi's eyes only, for she will be the only one this time who will know just how this note will read, unless she lets someone else read it."

"Oh okay, son. I thought it might have been something else that you were working on."

"That's okay. You didn't have any way of knowing, John."

"Son, when are you going to start writing you stories about your military career?"

"John, I have been thinking about getting with Mrs. John today and see if she has time to help in rewriting these."

"So you have been putting some down on paper."

"Yes, sir, I have. Do you think she will have time to help me rewrite them?"

"Son, you can only ask and see what she says."

"John, you can let me out at the coffee shop. I would like to talk with the captain about something."

"Okay, son. I will see you back at the shop. Do you want me to ask my sweet cake if she will help you?"

"Sure, here, take these with you. If she has time, she can start working on these."

"Okay, will do, Stash."

* * * * *

"Marianne, has the captain came by for lunch yet?"

"No, he has not come in yet."

"Well, I can wait until he comes in. There is something I need to talk with him about."

"Look, Stash, I would like to say I'm sorry about my behavior last night. I should have not come on to you the way I did."

"Marianne, there is nothing you need to be sorry for. You are a very attractive woman, and like I said, I was very tempted. But before I can enter into an intimate sexual relationship with any woman, I got to know in my own heart that I truly love her, and it must be in God's will because I once believe my first marriage was God's will and look how it turned out. Now can I get a cup of coffee?"

"Hey, Captain, over here. Here's the invoice for the rent on the trackhoe."

"Okay. Thanks, Stash, for all the help you have done with getting my ship back out to sea."

"No problem, Captain, glad I could be of help. What time are you planning on setting sail tomorrow? Currently, I'm not sure. Why?"

"Well, if I'm going to be aboard the ship when you set sail, I need to know the time."

"Okay, Stash. As soon as I know, I'll let you know."

"Okay, thanks, sir. I'll be waiting to hear from you. Marianne, thank you for the coffee. When you see Ms. Sue, tell her I said hello."

"Oh, you are welcome, and I appreciate you being honest with me earlier."

"Oh, you're welcome, Marianne."

MY UNIQUE ADVENTURES

I HAD BEEN OUT OF SCHOOL for about three or four mouths now, and was not sure where I was headed. Being new to the workforce and not knowing what type of job I wanted in life.

Well, one day, my oldest brother came home for his drill weekend. He asked me what I was going do with my life now that I had graduated from school. I told him that I had no idea what I was going to do, not having any type of work experience. He asked if I had thought about joining the military.

"Well, bro," I replied, "I had thought about joining the marines once back in school."

"Why would you want to join the marines?" he asked.

"Bro, it's because out of all the fighting forces who defend the constitution of our country and our way of life, I see them as being the best among the best."

"Well, why didn't you join the marines he asked?"

I told him that the recruiter called, asking for directions on how to get here. So I gave him the directions on how to get to the house. The very next day, he called back, asking once again on how to get here. He said that he was in the vicinity and wanted to stop by and talk. I asked, "Sir, just where are you again?" He began to tell me he was somewhere in Gulfport, Mississippi. I replied, "Sir, you're not in any way near where I live."

He said, "What do you mean I'm not near where you live? Don't you live here in Gulfport?"

"No, sir. I live in Waynesboro."

Well, he replied, "Sir, I went by the directions you gave me the day before."

I asked him, "Sir, just where was you coming from when you asked for directions?" He told me from his office over in Hattiesburg. I replied, "Sir, you didn't say yesterday that you would be coming from Hattiesburg when asking for directions. So, sir, I was under the impression that you would be coming from Laurel. Therefore, the directions I gave were from Laurel to Waynesboro, and not Hattiesburg to Waynesboro." Now as I was telling him this, I was thinking to myself, "Just how did he end up in Gulfport."

"Now, bro, you know that's why I didn't join the marines."

"Well, Clay, would you like to join the National Guard?"

"Well, bro, before I give you my answer, there this one question that I would like to ask."

"What would that be, Clay?"

"Bro, can the people in the National Guard give and take directions on where they are headed?"

He laughed and said, "Clay, why do you ask such a question as this?"

"Well, bro, if they're anything like the Marine that I talked to about joining and giving and taking directions where they're coming from or headed, then I'm not interested in joining because for once in this life, I would like to know where I'm headed."

"Well, would you like for me to set up a meeting with the recruiter for you?"

"Well, bro, you didn't answer my question."

"Now, littler brother, you know I can't answer such a question as this because we all make mistakes at some point in our lives."

"Yes, I know that, but mistakes such as this can cost someone their life."

"Yes, Clay, I know. Now do I set you up a meeting or not?"

"Well, I guess since I do need a part-time job." So he set up a date and time for me to meet with the recruiter. I went and met the recruiter on the date that they had set up. The recruiter began to tell me all kinds of stuff that would become available to me once I joined the National Guard, such things as a signing bonus if I scored high enough on the (ASVAB) test, and the GI Bill that would pay for college if I chose to go back to school for a higher education. As he was telling me about all these benefits on joining, I was thinking, "Hey, now this might not be all that bad of an idea after all."

I sure could use the extra cash to buy my own place, but as for the GI Bill, well, I didn't see myself going back to school anytime soon. Now just for laughter, who in their right mind would want go back to school after spending fifteen years of their life trying to get out of school, just to go back for another eight years?

"Clay, he says the first step in becoming a member of the military is to pass the (ASVAB) test."

I was thinking to myself, "Now I'm not any good on taking tests. I didn't like them back in school, and to this day, I don't like taking them. But oh well, I'm going to take this one and give it my all on passing it."

He put the test in front of me and said, "You have one hour to complete this test." Now he was telling me that I got a time limit in taking this test. Man, that was even worst. Well, the hour was up. He returned, took my test, and put his answer sheet on top of the test to see if I had passed it.

He looked at me, shaking his head, and said, "I'm sorry to inform you, but it looks as if you didn't pass this test." My head just dropped in disbelief. I just knew I had passed the test. He looked back down once more at his answer sheet and said. "Oh wait, Clyde, my bad. I had the answer sheet upside down. By the way, congratulations. Once we get you sworn in, you will be on your way of becoming a member of the National Guard."

I looked at him, wanting to give him a piece of my mind on what I was thinking, but I just bit my tongue instead.

Now I was in the National Guard. My first day at drill, they were all standing in formation for roll call. When the first sergeant was done calling roll, he called for me to come out in front of the company. He said, "I would like to introduce our newest member in the unit. Everyone, this is Private Clyde."

I looked at him and asked, "Why are you calling me Clyde?"

He replied, "That's what the recruiter called you. Now is this not your name?" (This was the first time I questioned my brother after I joined. Could these folks not remember my name?)

"No, sir. That is not my name. My name is Private Mills."

He looked at me and said, "Don't you ever address me with 'sir.' I'm only the first sergeant. I'm not the commanding officer. For you only address officers with 'sir.'" He then asked, "What does the C stand for, if not for Clyde?"

"Well, First Sergeant, it's my middle initial, which stands for Clay."

He said, "Private Mills, go and stand behind the third platoon formation."

I was like, "Okay. Now just which one is third platoon?"

He pointed to the group standing closest to the front door. He then ordered the platoon sergeant to take charge of their soldiers and get them to work. As the platoon sergeant showed me around the armory, he introduced me to the people in his platoon. They would in return explain to me the type of work I would be doing once I became Military Occupational Specialty (MOS) qualified. That entailed going off to basic training and Advanced Individual Training (AIT). Now until I became MOS qualified, the platoon sergeant would not let me put my hands on any of the equipment. They would only let me watch themselves operate their equipment. "Hands off, Clyde. Not today, you aren't!"

"Man, I'm enjoying this. I can't wait until I get MOS qualified for I can play with these new toys. Whoops, did I just say 'toys'? I meant to say 'work with this equipment.' My bad, platoon sergeant."

"Oh, good, it's now lunch time, and I will get to try some of this good military food that the cooks have prepared for us. The first sergeant said since I was the newest recruit, I could be the first to go in line to be served. Boy, I'm thinking this is nice of everyone to let me be first in line for I'm hungry enough I could eat a pot of hog chitterlings." But what I didn't know was that I was being set up. I got my plate and walked up to the first person. He put a spoonful on my plate, and the next one put a spoonful on top of that one. I was thinking, "Now what is this all about?" Then the next person did the same. By the time I got to the end of the line, all my food was in one big pile. As I was walking away, I looked back at them with a smile and said, "I would have liked my food to be separated, but hey, food is food, right?"

Day 2 was more like the first. Except today, I had more paperwork to fill out, and I also got to order my first set of military uniforms. I knew they were going to look great on me. I had been told before by some women that I looked great in camouflage, just to let you know. "Now Clyde," I thought, "it's because they couldn't see you (ha-ha)." The following drill weekend, my platoon sergeant informed me that they were going to teach me how to do what they called drill and ceremony. I was like, "Okay, just what is drill and ceremony?" He told me it was where you learn how to march as a unit while in formation and do face movement in unity. Man, I'm telling you, by the time we got done with this block of instruction on becoming a soldier, I didn't know my right foot from my left or my right arm from the left with all the right flank march, left flank march, then rear march; counter column; left face, right face present arms. I was like which arm: order arms, open ranks, close ranks, right face, file from the left column left march. And then all at once, there came gas, gas. I was like, "What (gas, gas)? Oh, just never mind, Clyde, for this will end this block of instructions on how to become a soldier."

Now let's move on to the next block of instructions. "Private Mills, in this classroom block of instruction, you will learn how to distinguish the difference between the ranks of leadership. Then after lunch, we will show you once again how drill and ceremony are done. But this time, we'll be using our weapons and gas mask."

I was thinking, "Okay, this is going to be fun to see this go around because I like to know just what this thing, they call a gas mask is really used for." Hmm, now just what type of gas are you thinking it's used for? Oh no, it's not used for what you may be thinking. Although, it could be used for that, if such gas is potent enough.

* * * * *

"Now, John, may I continue my story?"

"Clyde, what you say we take a coffee break before moving on to the next classroom block of instruction?"

"I'm thinking now why it's so hard for you people to remember that my name is not Clyde."

"Oh yes! Sir, I could use a nice cup of coffee right now."

"I'm feeling that strange look once again, just like the one I got from the first sergeant when I addressed him as 'sir.'

* * * * *

"If I don't learn anything else this drill weekend, it's got to be that you don't address an enlisted person as 'sir.' Clyde, in this classroom block of instruction, you will learn how to orient yourself by using a map."

I was thinking, *Okay, now you have really got me lost with this.* "You want me to use this map here to orient myself on where I'm at in life. Now I got to say this has been one interesting and busy weekend. One I won't forget for some time to come because I'm now more confused than ever before and am lost where I'm now at in life."

"Well, now, Private Clyde, it's time to end another drill weekend. But before we dismiss today; there is just one more thing I need your help with."

"Okay, Sergeant. What do you need my help with?"

"First Sergeant has asked that you do a police call around the compound before I can dismiss you for the day."

I started scratching my head thinking, "Hmm, now why does he need me to do a police call around the compound? Could it be that there is someone else here as lost as I am. Oh well, I'll do whatever it takes to get out of here for the day."

I went around the compound doing these police call, not knowing for sure just what I was supposed to be doing. It was not until someone stopped me and asked, "Private Clyde, what you are doing?"

I replied, "A police call." He then explained to me just what a police call consisted of. I looked at him with a look to say, "Hmm, you don't say."

* * * * *

"Now, son, just what does a police call consist of?"

"John, I'm glad you asked. A police call is where you pick things up from off the ground that does not grow. Now, John, before we move on with my journey back through the times of me becoming a member of the unit, what you say that we take an intermission and get a bite to eat?"

"Clyde, that's a great idea." "

"John, my name is not Clyde. Now stop calling me that. John, before our next drill came around, I received this phone call from the Readiness NCO."

* * * * *

Someone from Readiness NCO informed me that he needed me to come by the armory. He had some information he needed to give me on when and where I was going for my basic training in the summer. I got to the armory and he began to inform me that I would be going to Fort Jackson, South Carolina, for my basic training. He also told me I could either fly out of Pine Belt airport over in Hattiesburg, or I could go to Jackson airport and fly from there to Atlanta, Georgia, and then on to South Carolina. I would go and ask, "Is this another test in which if I don't choose the correct airport, it could mean I don't get to go?"

He laughed and said, "It's only a multiple-choice test, and no, you can't get it wrong even if you tried."

"Sir, that's good because I'm going to choose to fly from Hattiesburg."

"Clyde, you do know how to get there, right?"

"Sir, I've been looking forward to this good news for some time. Now I'm just an old backwoods country boy, who has never flown on an airplane before. I will say the only type of flying I had ever done before was when I accidentally fell out of a pine tree as a young boy. My brother and two of our cousins were trying to see just which one of us could climb the farthest when a limb broke and down I went. Man, I got to tell you that flight didn't go all that well."

He said, "Now, Clyde, when I get the informant on what date and time you are to report to the airport, I'll give you a call."

"Sir, I'll be waiting for your call then." These were just the beginnings of some of my first footsteps of becoming a soldier in the Mississippi National Guard, in which I have come to appreciate and love as a seasoned soldier.

* * * * *

"John, did you read any of this when he gave it to you?"

"No ma'am, I didn't have the time. I had to drive going there and coming back. Why do you ask?"

"Well, John, it looks like he has started writing about his time of being in the armed forces."

"Mom, that is great news. I have been asking him for some time now to tell us about some of his adventures as a service member in the military. Mom, what do you think about what he has writing so far?"

"Well John, so far, from what I have read of it, it's sounding pretty good, but you need to read it for yourself and see if you understand any of it."

"Well, okay, give it here and I will give it a good look over for myself and see if he has any mistakes that need correcting."

"Now, John, that was not a very nice thing to say because you know he is not as well educated as some people are. Besides it's not his fault he was born tongue-tied and has trouble putting his sentences in proper order. I think he has come a long way in life with having to overcome such an adversity as this. You know he has struggled with this all his life. John, there's just one more thing. As I recall, you were not all *that* smart with your language either. And I also recall you had to have a tutor to help you. Now put that in your pipe and smoke on *that*, why don't you?"

"Now hold on, Mom, you need to calm down a little. I didn't mean for it to sound the way you took it. I was just saying he may need some help in some areas, that's all."

"Well John, you know it's one of my pet peeves. I just don't like to hear someone talk down on other people because of their differences."

"Well, Mom, I'm sorry, okay? If it will help to make you feel better, I like the way he starts his story off with the title he has chosen."

"Oh yes, so do I, John, but I cannot help to wonder why he chose to use a subtitle."

"Now, Mom, you're going to have to ask him that when he gets back from meeting with the captain."

"John, why is he meeting with the captain today?"

"He said something about not having enough money to pay all the rent that was left, owing on the trackhoe. He was going to ask him if he would pay the remaining portion of the rent since it was used to dig a channel around the ship."

"Well, John, how much did he say was left owing on the rent?"

"Mom, I'm think he may have said something like around two thousand or somewhere that amount."

"Wow, John, around two thousand, you don't say."

"Mary, now that's what he had said. I didn't go in the shop with him. Therefore, I don't know." "John, I'm just wondering why they still owe that much. Have they not been making their monthly payments on time?

"Mom, I don't know if the captain has been helping with his part of the payment for the work. I only know that Son has been putting all he has, on his part of the bill, along with Mr. Mac. Mr. Mac has been helping some with the engineer's portion of the bill."

"John, now just who is this person you're calling Mr. Mac?"

"Mary, Mr. Mac is the older gentleman who made room in his home for Son and his wildflower Jimi when they first arrived here in Sandspur."

"Well, John, why is he paying part of the bill?"

"Mary, according to what Son told me when he came to stay here with me at the shop, Mr. Mac is also the co-owner of the ship along with Mr. Floyd."

"Now, John, just who is Mr. Floyd?"

"Oh, Mary, now Mr. Floyd is the captain of the ship. Now will there be anything else that you would like to know before I go back to work?"

"Well, yes, there is just one more thing." "What would that be, Mary?"

"John, just where do you plan on sleeping tonight, using that tone of voice with me?"

"Oh, Mom, I'm planning on sleeping with you. Have you forgotten that we are still on our honeymoon, and you know that you still light up my firecracker?"

"Oh, John, you crazy ole man. Get out of here and go to work." "Yes, ma'am. I love you, my little hot box."

"John, you better go now before you get something started that you can't finish."

"Mom, you know that I can finish everything I start."

"Yeah, right, John. You best be going before I prove you wrong, and you know that I can."

"Mary, we will just see tonight who can prove who wrong."

"John, go do your work."

"Mary, I'm trying my best, but you keep telling me that you're going to prove me wrong."

"John, just go, okay, before Son comes in and finds you acting the way you are."

"Well, if he has never seen anyone…well, never mind. I'll be going."

* * * * *

"Good evening, Ms. Mary. How are you?"

"Son, I would like to know just one thing."

"What would that be, Ms. Mary?"

"Is Mr. Floyd going to pay the remaining two thousand dollars owing on the bill?"

"Ms. Mary, would you mind backing up for just a minute and explain to me what you are talking about here?"

"Son, John said that you had to go meet with Mr. Floyd about what was left owing on the bill."

"Ms. Mary, now just who in the heck is this Mr. Floyd that you are speaking of?"

"Now, son, according to what John told me earlier, Mr. Floyd is the captain and co-owner of the ship, along with Mr. Mac, who has been helping you pay the engineers for their work in getting the ship back out into the ocean in order for you to continue on your new adventure in life searching for your new wildflower."

"Oh, okay. Now that I know who Mr. Floyd is, can you please tell me who this Mr. Mac is that you just spoke of as being the co-owner of the ship?"

"Now, Stash—oh Son, I'm sorry. I didn't mean to call you Stash."

"Ms. Mary, that's quite all right. I've been called a lot worse than Stash before."

"Well, son, you have been here now going on six months and you don't know who Mr. Mac is?"

"No, ma'am, I don't. Sorry."

"Well, Mr. Mac is the one who gave you and Jimi a place to stay at his home when you two first came to Sandspur."

"Oh, now I understand why he was so willing to help pay a part of the bill for the work that the engineers have done on the ship. Hmm, he is also the father of Mr. Slick Cool-Pepper who went and swept Ms. Jimi off her feet at the very first chance he got. I just hope and pray he will love her in the way she deserves to be loved by a man. You know, Ms. Mary, in the way that Mr. John loves you, and you love him."

"Yes, son. I know she means a lot to you, and you only want the very best for her. But you need to get on with your life and forget about her. She has made her choice in life on who she wants to be with."

"Yes, ma'am, you are right as always."

"Ha-ha, you know it, son. I'm always right. Just ask John."

"Yep, right. Ha ha. I do need to be moving on with my lonely messed up life. But before I do move on to my next journey in life searching this world over for my one true soul mate, I would like for just once to be able to find a very lovely way to show her how much I appreciated her for what she has done for me."

"Son, can I just ask why do you feel that you need to show her anything at all?"

"Well, Mary, I have never met a woman quite like her before. She makes me feel as if I can take the world head on with no problems whatsoever. She just seems to have that kind of power over me, unlike any other women who I have met so far on this ole rugged journey in which I have found myself to be on, looking for my soul mate."

"Okay, son, I understand that. And I know that we don't often meet someone who can make us feel that way about ourselves. I felt that way when I first met John back in school, forty-eight years ago. Now let's be moving on to what you had asked John to give me to look over for you. Before we do, did you get the yellow and red rose you went after?"

"No, ma'am. They didn't have any. She said that they would have some in about three weeks."

"Are you going to stay another month and see if you can get one to give Ms. Sue? She just may be divorced by then, or you can get one for Marianne. You did say that she finds you to be attractive."

"Ms. Mary, not to sound rude or anything, I prefer not to talk about either one of them right now, okay? But to answer your question, yes, I do plan on staying until the next ship comes in. That's if you and Mr. John don't mind."

"Son, you know that we don't mind you staying. John has already said you could stay if you like. You know that he loves having you around here, helping him in the shop, and I too love having you here. You have made our lives around here just a little more interesting."

"Thank you, Mary. To be truthful with you, I'm starting to love being around you both also. You both have been so helpful to me while I've been waiting for the ship to set sail once again. I don't know how I will ever be able to repay you both for giving me a place to stay and food to eat."

"Now, son, you know that John and I are very thankful to God for allowing us to be able to help those who need help."

"Well, Ms. Mary, I was thinking on my way here that I could continue to write about my time in the military. You know that John has been wanting me to tell him about some of those unique adventures which I'm very grateful to have had the opportunity to be a part of as a seasoned soldier. So what do you think about what I've written so far?"

"Well, son, from what I have read so far, you seem to be telling some great stories about your time as a soldier. John and I like the title that you came up with, but we were just wondering why you have a subtitle."

"Well now, Ms. Mary, that is a good question, and you do have the right to know. But I'm not going to tell you the answer at this time because I would like for Mr. John to hear my answer as well."

"Well, son, I understand, but you don't owe us any kind of explanation why you chose to use a subtitle."

"Well, Ms. Mary, did John say when he would be back?"

"No, he didn't, son."

"I am wondering, could he still be over at Mork and Mendy? What did he go over there for? Oh never mind, Ms. Mary. He told me he was going to take Mork the part for the motorcycle he picked up in Seaport today. Ms. Mary, can I ask you a question?"

"Sure, son, what's on your mind? Oh, son, I'm sorry. Let me answer the phone before you ask me your question. It might be John.

"Okay, Son that was John. He said to ask you if you don't mind going into the shop and pick up a solenoid and a set of new plugs and bring them over to Mork's at his shop. He needs them to finish the work on his old bike that he has been restoring."

"Did he say which solenoid and plugs to get?"

"Son, he said that the solenoid and plugs are on the bottom shelf by the cash register. Now what is the question that you wanted to ask me?"

"What is one of the hardest lesson would you say that you had to learn to overcome in life?"

"Wow. Now, son, that is a very good question. Hmm, hardest lesson you ask. I'm going to say I will have to get back with you on that one. I'm going to need some time to think that one over, okay?"

"Well, I guess that I need to head over to Mork's with these parts before John calls back with an attitude wanting to know where I'm at."

"Okay, son. I will try to have you an answer by the time you get back."

* * * * *

"John, here are the parts you asked for."

"Well, take them over to Mork. He is the one who is working on the bike, not me."

As I was watching Mork install the parts on his 1982 Honda bike, I remembered my 1981 Honda CB 750 custom that was given to me by a friend for my service to our country. I missed riding that old bike. It was the first bike that my ex-wife and I took our first ride on together before our first child was born.

"Son, what are you smiling about now?"

"John, I was just thinking back in time when I took my ex-wife for her first ride on a motorcycle."

"Son, how did she like the ride, it being her first time on the back of a bike?"

"Well, John, I guess she loved it. She wanted me to go buy one, but there was no way at the time we could afford one.

"Mork, can I ask you and John something?"

"Yep, I guess so. What's on your mind?"

"What would you say would be one of the hardest lesson in life that you had to learn to overcome?"

"Hmm, that's a very hard question to answer for there has been a lot of adversities that I have had to face in my life over the past few years."

"What about you, Dad? What would you say has been the hardest lesson for you?"

"Mork, the hardest lesson for me would be learning how to be both mom and dad to you and your brother. Being a single parent raising children is hard. When you mom passed, I had no idea on how I was going to take care of y'all by myself."

"Dad, I may not have ever told you this before, but you did a great job at taking care of Jim and me. And I will never forget that, Dad, as long as I live."

"Well, thank you, son. I do appreciate you saying that for I always try my very best to do what I feel was the right thing to do by you both. Mork, now what is your answer to Son's question?"

"Well, I'm going to say my hardest lesson would be not to trust people again after they had lied to me more than once. Now, Stash, why are you asking this question?"

"Mork, I was just wondering how many different answers I would get from people. John, I'm going to head on back to the shop. There is something that I need to write down for my next book."

"Wait, son, you can leave the bike here tonight and ride home with me. There is something I would like to talk to you about if you don't mind. Just let me say goodnight to my grandson Mark then I'll be ready."

I was thinking now just what he wanted to talk with me about. "Okay, Mr. John. I'll be waiting in the truck."

* * * * *

"Son, what I want to talk to you about is what you have written so far for you new book. The first thing I would like to know is why are you using a subtitle."

"Well, John, when we get back to the shop, I'll tell you both."

"What do you mean tell us both?"

"Well, Mrs. John asked me that same question earlier. I told her that I would answer it only when I could tell you both at the same time. Now is there anything else you would like to know?"

"Well, I guess not since you seem to be getting an attitude with me asking you questions."

"No, Mr. John. I don't have a problem with you asking me why I chose to use a subtitle. I wanted to tell you both, that is all. Now I would like to know what you think about it so far."

"Son, I like the part about the drill and ceremony where you said present arms, order arms, which arm. And then you said something about gas, gas. Now that was funny. When are you going to tell us about your basic training experience at Fort Jackson, South Carolina?”

"John, I got to tell about my experience of going through the airport first.”

"Now, son, I'm going to look forward to hearing about your adventure about the airport.”

"John, it was a doozy for this backwoods country boy who has never flown before.”

"Son, do you even know what the definition of ‘doozy’ is?”

"Yeah, John. I did get a little more educational when I went through basic training—them drill sergeants at Fort Jackson has seen to that.”

"Son, I hate to hurt your feelings here, but they didn't do a very good job at educational you.”

"Oh, you don't say, John. You can't even get the correct definition of which word to use, either ‘education,’ ‘educating,’ or ‘educational.’ Now, Mr. Know-It-All, who is educated?”

"John, what are you two arguing about now?”

Oh, Mom, we were just talking about his experience at basic training.”

"Can I get you both a cup of coffee?”

"Yes, Mary, I would love a cup.”

"Here's your coffee. Now, son, you said that you would tell us why you decided to use a subtitle for your book.”

"Okay, Mrs. John, why I decided to use a subtitle is that the stories are not going to be in any particular order. Now if you don't mind, I'm going to say good night and go see just what story I can come up with. But before I go, Mrs. John, I would like to know your answer to my question I asked you earlier.”

"Well, son, to answer your question, I would say it's learning how to forgive others who has done me wrong in life. Now, son, I would like to know your answer.”

"Now, Mrs. John, my answer would be somewhat like yours.”

"Son, I don't understand why you say it's somewhat like my answer?”

"Mrs. John, I find it very hard to overlook someone who looks down their nose at someone who may or may not be as well educated as they think themselves to be. I know myself not to be as well educated as most people are in this world, but I do know this: we are not to think of ourselves to be better than anyone else for God has created us all in his own image."

"Amen, son, you just said a mouthful."

"Now, John, see, I'm not the only one who don't like people looking down their nose at other people for their inability."

LEAVING HOME FOR
BASIC TRAINING

THE TIME HAVE FINALLY COME for me to leave home to make my travel into an unknown world, my military training at Fort Jackson. My stepdad and mom took me to the airport for a four-month vacation. Well, I thought it was going to be anyway. My first time ever being on an airplane was when I flew from Pine Belt airport to Atlanta, Georgia, on my way to South Carolina for my basic training. The Pine Belt airport was not at all a big airport, so I didn't have a hard time getting to where I needed to be to catch my flight out to Atlanta.

The time have finally come for me to leave home to make my travel into an unknown world, my military training at Fort Jackson. My stepdad and mom took me to the airport for a four-month vacation. Well, I thought it was going to be anyway. My first time ever being on an airplane was when I flew from Pine Belt airport to Atlanta, Georgia, on my way to South Carolina for my basic training. The Pine Belt airport was not at all a big airport, so I didn't have a hard time getting to where I needed to be to catch my flight out to Atlanta.

I gripped the armrest, holding on for dear life. Hmm, yep, right? Like this was going to help keep us from falling out of the sky and hitting the ground. Well, somewhere about halfway to Atlanta, the flight attendant came around and asked if I would like something to drink. My reply was, "Yes, please, after that heart-wrenching scare

y'all just gave me about five minutes ago. I would like a cup of ___."
Just for fun, I'm going to let you fill in the blank space on what you may think I would have asked for being this was my first time ever flying. Outside, of course, from the time I got thrown out of the back of the pickup and the time I fell out of the tree. Oh, I'm sorry. You don't know the story behind that. I talked about that in my first book, when my stepdad got killed in the wreck.

We got to Atlanta airport. I got off the plane and started looking around for my next gate to board my connecting flight to South Carolina. Now Atlanta, Georgia's airport was way bigger than Pine Belt. One could get lost easily and miss their flight if they didn't know just where they needed to go to catch their connecting flight. It was as if they put you off on one side of the airport just for this very reason, for I had to go slam across the other side of the airport to get to my connecting flight to South Carolina. I do now understand why you have hours on hours of layovers at times. It's to give you time to find your connecting flight and get something to eat and drink from all the walking you just did just to get to your next gate. Now this plane I was getting on was much bigger than the first plane I was on coming here, and the flight to South Carolina was nowhere as bad as the first one that I was on to Atlanta.

I got to South Carolina, and there once again, I found myself looking around for someone to tell me where I should go to find someone who was to take me to Fort Jackson. I finally found someone who told me where I needed to go. As I made my way there, I was looking around the airport just in case I needed to find my way back one day. I began to wander just what I have gotten myself into here, for this country boy has never been outside of Mississippi on his own before. As I was waiting at the bus stop, there came this other person who asked, "Are you waiting on a bus to go to Fort Jackson?"

I replied, "Yes, I am. What about you?"

He replied, "Yes, sir, I am. I'm going there for my boot camp training."

"May I ask just where you are from, private?"

He replied with this great big old smile on his face, "Sir, I'm glad you asked me. I'm from good ole sweet home Alabama. What about you?" he asked.

"I'm from God's country as well, the beautiful state of Mississippi, where we are also talked to show respect for all people. Now are you regular army or National Guard?"

"I'm regular army," he replied. "My dad and his father were regular army, so I figured after I finished high school and all, you see."

As he was telling me this, I was thinking to myself, "I just thought I was a backwoods county boy."

He continued, "I would just follow in their footsteps and carry on an old family tradition in serving my God and country. What about you?"

"Oh, I joined the National Guard back in my hometown of Waynesboro. I somehow or another let my oldest brother talk me into joining. In his closing statement, he pointed out the fact that I could use the extra money to help pay my bills. So I'm here now, awaiting to become a well-trained member of our country's greatest fighting force ever. I think we are, anyway."

As we continued to talk, there were more people starting to show up and joining our conversation about being a member of the military. After about thirty minutes of waiting around, a bus pulled up from Fort Jackson and off came this guy with a Smokey the Bear hat on. He said, "I'm here to see that you all get to Fort Jackson for your boot camp training. Before you get on my bus, I need to see a copy of your orders." So they went digging in their bags for the orders. Just so happened I had mine in my hand. I gave him a copy, and he replied, "Get on the bus and go all the way to back. Take a seat and keep your mouth shut, private." Man, I'm telling you, I thought that I lost the butterflies on the flight here, but somehow, they must have found their way back into my stomach once again for they were cutting up like they never have before. We finally got to where we were going, and the bus driver opened that door on the bus.

* * * * *

"Mrs. John, before you call it a night, would you mind looking over this and telling me what you think on how I could make it more interesting to read?"

"No, son, give it here. You know that I would love to look over what you have written. Son, so far, what I have read looks good, but before I make any recommendations on how I think you can improve on what you have written here, may I ask why are you saying it in the way that you are?" "Well, Mrs. John, I'm just trying to tell my stories and use a bit of humor, you know, to make them sound funnier to the readers. That's all. Why, do you not find it amusing?"

"Oh no, son, that's not it at all. I can see why you want to use a little sense of humor in telling your story. May I ask, son, why you stopped with it here?"

"What do you mean, Mrs. John?"

"Well, you stopped when he opened the door on the bus."

"Well, I stopped there because I was tired. My little old brain just couldn't work anymore overtime like it did when I was…oh, just never mind. Good night.

"Good night, son. Hope you get a good night's sleep. See you in the morning."

"Okay, thanks. Same to you both. I'm going to read my Bible before I call it a night."

"Mom, I was beginning to think he would never go to bed. Now we can pick up from where we left off earlier today."

"Now, John, you know he has not yet went to sleep. He can still hear what is going on."

"What? Did you say something to me, Mrs. John?"

"No, son. I was just talking to John."

"Oh, okay then. Good night."

"See now? I told you, John. He can hear you, so you need to keep your moaning and groaning down to a minimum when your firecracker is on fire and is about to explode like a stick of dynamite."

"Oh, Mom, I never in my wildest dreams thought that you felt it like a stick of dynamite."

"Well, John, I'm just trying to build up your confidence a little. You need all the help that I can give you, my one and only true love."

"Now, Mom, you know just by you being in my arms is all the confidence that this old boy will ever need. Now come your beautiful self here and give me a kiss, and let's see if we can get that spark started."

"John, did you hear that?"

"Hear what, Mom?"

"It sounded like someone was knocking at the door."

"Well, maybe if we just ignore the knock, whoever it is will go away."

"Now, John, that is no way to be. I'm going to see who it may be now. Are you going to come with me or not?"

"Hmm, I guess so."

* * * * *

"Good evening, Ms. Jimi. Come on in. What are you doing out so late?"

"Mrs. John, I heard that Son was going to be leaving tomorrow on the ship to start his new journey in life. I've been trying to think of a way to tell him how I feel about our friendship and what the yellow and red rose meant to me the day he had them sent to me along with the note."

"Yes, Jimi. I heard about him sending you the rose. That was so sweet of him."

"Yes, ma'am. He really touched my heart in the way he wrote the note explaining what each item represented. Now is he here?"

"Yes, he is in his room. But before you go in to see him, I need to let you know he is reading his Bible and that he is going to stay just until the next ship comes back in."

"Well, I guess if he is going to stay a little longer, I will meet with him another day. Oh, by the way, please don't say anything to him about me stopping by tonight."

"Okay, Jimi. We won't. Good night.

* * * * *

As I read the book of Isaiah chapter 41, I came up on these verses, and I began to think back on how long I've been in this desolate place, in search of that one true love. For these words gave my heart new hope in just knowing that if I will just wait upon the Lord my God, he will surely renew my strength.

Being of the flesh, we sometime have the tendency to think that we must have everything we want within an hour. Oh, how easy it is to forget as humans that one day in God's eyes is as a thousand years. Lord my God, hear me, O Lord as I lay myself down to sleep. Lord, if it be within your love and will to reach down from your heavenly throne and renew my strength, that I may find it within my own spiritual walk to become a much better servant to you. Lord, not my own will in which you gave unto me to do as I so choose, but that of your own will to be done within my life as you so choose for it to be done within my best interest. Thank you, O Lord.

Good night, and may God keep his loving hands around us all.

> He giveth power to the faint; and to them that have no might he increaseth strength. Even the youths shall faint and be weary, and the young men shall utterly fall: But they that wait upon the Lord shall renew their strength; they shall mount up with wings as eagles; they shall run, and not be weary; and they shall walk, and not faint. (Isa. 41:29–31, KJV)

* * * * *

"Good morning, Mr. John. How are you and Mrs. John this morning?"

"Son, it's way too early to say. I have not had my morning coffee. Will you please get me a cup and add a small shot to it? I got a headache. Mary wore me out with all the fireworks last night. Just when I thought we were about done, she would light up again."

"Do what, Mr. John"?

"Son, don't play dumb with me. You know what I'm talking about."

"Hmm, what may I ask were you two celebrating?"

"Son, we were celebrating our two-month anniversary."

"Hmm, I'm thinking to myself now that explains all the moaning and groaning, and 'Oh yeah baby, I'm loving the fireworks.'"

"Now, son, I can tell you that woman knows how to celebrate unlike any other woman I've ever met before. Now can you get me another cup of coffee, and this time add two shots to it? That first cup didn't get the job done. My head is still throbbing. You can also add some to yours if you like."

"No, thanks, I'm good with just black coffee. John, would you like me to fix you something to eat?"

"No, son. Mary will do that when she gets up. All I need right now is my strong cup of coffee. Son, did you work on your book last night?"

"No, sir, I didn't. I just have not been in the right frame of mind to do any writing here lately. After getting to the reception station, I'm not sure just which way I want to go with my story."

"Well, son, may I say just write down whatever comes to mind as you have in the past, and let Mary and myself look over it for you? You know that we don't mind helping you out. Mary has said more than once how she loves the way you tell your stories."

"Well, John, that's very kind of you. If I get time today, I would like to take a walk down to the ocean and just let my mind run free and see what I can come up with."

"Son, you can take the day off from the shop if you would like and work on your book."

"Thank you, sir. I believe I will do just that."

"Son, before you go, I would like to ask you something."

"Sure, John. What's on your mind?"

"Son, there was this question that was asked of me some time back, and for some reason, it has been bothering me on how I answered it."

"Well now, John, what is the question?

"Son, it's not as much as the question within itself that is bothering me, it's the way in which I answered it."

"Okay, John, just how did you answer the question?"

"I told the person that it's not my opinion that matters. It's God's opinion that matters in such a situation as theirs."

"John, I got to say you have got me lost here by you telling someone that it's not your opinion that matters, but it's God's opinion that matters."

"Son, you know that I do confess to be a born-again Christian. Now as a born-again Christian, I feel that I have failed God in sharing his word with this person about the ungodly lifestyle in which they are living. What if this person was to die today, not knowing that the lifestyle is abomination in God's eyes? By me not explaining unto this person the truth of God's word, I have now failed within my own belief. Shouldn't we have enough courage within our own belief in God that we are able to explain unto others why we believe in God the way we do, and are we not to be a good steward of God's word and be ready to take the world face on whenever it comes against God's teaching?"

"John, I don't know how to answer all your questions here, but I got to say I do agree with you on the part about having enough confidence in our own beliefs in taking the world face on."

"Thank you, son, for this has been eating at me for some time now. I just hope from here on out that I will be a better servant for God."

"Oh, good morning, Mrs. John. How are you?"

"Good morning, son. I'm doing just fine. How about yourself?"

"I'm doing great, Mrs. John. Thank you."

"Would you boys like for me to fix you something to eat?"

"No, ma'am, I'm good. Thanks though. I was about to head down to the diner to see if Ms. Sue is working today."

"Well okay, son. See you when you get back."

"Son, I thought you were going down to the ocean to work on your book."

"John, I'm going to, but I'm going to see if Sue would like to go with me. That's if she can take the time off."

* * * * *

"Good morning, Marianne. Is Sue working today?"

"Why? Is there something wrong, Stash?"

"Oh no, there's nothing wrong, Marianne. I just need to talk to her. Now is she here?"

"Well, Stash, if that's the way you're going to be."

"Whoops, I'm so sorry, Marianne. How are you today?"

"Now, Stash, that is much better. And yes, you need to be sorry with your handsome self. Now to answer you, yes, Sue is working. She is filling in for one of our cooks who called and said he's going to be late today. Now is there something that I can help you with?"

"Marianne, I just wanted to see if either one of y'all could take the day off and spend it on the beach with me."

"Stash, you know that I would love to take the day off and spend it with you on the beach. Just let me go and ask the manager if it will be okay for me to do so. Would you like me to get you a cup of coffee while you wait?"

"Well, maybe a half a cup. Thank you, Marianne."

"Okay, here's your coffee, and don't go anywhere. I will be right by, okay?"

"Hey, Stash, what brings you down here to the diner this early? Shouldn't you be aboard the ship?"

"Oh hello, Sue. Lady, you are looking great today."

"Thank you, Stash. That's very nice of you to say."

"Well, I just call it as I see it, beautiful."

"Now to answer your question. No, I've decided to stay until the next supply ship comes in before I start a new journey out on the open sea."

"Well, Stash, I'm glad you decided to stay a little longer. Maybe we can get to know each other a little better."

"Yes, I would like that myself, Sue, but you are still married and that plays a big part in us spending some time with each other."

"Stash, is there anything I can get you?"

"No, Sue, I'm good for now, thanks."

"Okay, I got to get back in the kitchen. Hope to see you later."

"Sorry, Stash, she said that I couldn't take the day off, but I could have tomorrow off if you want me to."

"Well, okay. I'll get back with you about tomorrow, Marianne."

* * * * *

"Hold on now, son. Are you telling me that you can't have long hair or a mustache in the army?"

"No, John. Not in basic training, you can't."

* * * * *

He asked, "Why then do you have one, private? The next time I see you, it best be gone. Do you understand?"

We went inside, and he told us that we would be here about two weeks, getting our medical examinations and shots. Once we were done with that, we would be issued our battle dress uniform (BDU) and physical training (PT) uniform, and then fitted for our Class A and B dress uniform. After getting our wall lockers scratched away, he showed us all just once how to make our beds the army way.

The next day, we went to the barbershop. The barber asked, "How much would you like for me to cut off, Son?"

"Oh, not that much, sir," I replied.

I'm telling you by the time he was done, I had no hair on my head or on my face. Well, time has come for us to go to our company to begin our training. We would get up at 4:00 a.m. for PT. We would start out with some stretching exercises for warm up, and then came the pushups, sit ups, the dying cockroach, mountain climbing, and then the two-mile run. There this one morning, our drill sergeant was leading the PT run. They had these water cans sitting around the track. He started running backward for some reason and ran right into the water cans. Now before this took place, he fell off the platform.

* * * * *

"Son, why did he fall off the PT platform?"

"John, I guess he didn't realize just how close he was to the edge when he gave the command front leaning rest position move. He went down, and right off the platform he went."

"Did he get hurt?"

"No, not that we knew of. But at the same time, we didn't get to finish any more of the warm up exercises that we were doing."

"What did you all do next, Son?"

* * * * *

Another drill sergeant took over and we continued with the exercises. When we were done, we went to eat breakfast. They didn't give us much time to eat. They said that we had a lot of training to do today and part of that training was going to the gas chamber. Now this was where I learned what a gas mask was really used for. They took us into this tent and they told us before we could get out of the tent that we had to take off our masks and say our names. Before I could say my name, the gas hit my face, and it had me gasping for air. My nose was running, my eyes burning, but I was still able to say my name and they let me out. What I didn't know was that just outside the tent, there was a pine tree that we all ran right into.

* * * * *

"Son, why did you run into the tree?"

"John, if you had ever been in a gas chamber before, you would understand what teargas would do to a person. It will have your eyes burning, and your nose running. It will clear out your sinuses. We were done with the gas chamber and went on to the next part."

"What part of you training did you all do next, Son?"

"John, if you would stop interrupting me, I will tell you."

* * * * *

We went marching back to the barracks. The drill sergeant had us calling cadence.

* * * * *

"Son, what is 'cadence'?"

"Well, John, it's a song sung that serves the purpose of keeping soldiers "dress, right, dress," moving in step as a unit while in formation, while maintaining the correct beat or cadence."

* * * * *

We went to the supply room and drew our weapons to go to the zero range and then on to the qualification range.

* * * * *

"Wait now, John, before you go and ask. The zero and qualification range is where we learn how to fire the M16."

* * * * *

The next thing we did was to learn how to move under direct fire of a machine gun and move from one hasty fighting position to the next while under live fire. Once we were done qualifying, we had to break the weapon down and clean them. Getting it cleaned took some time. There were places on the weapon that you couldn't get to without having a special tool.

The next day, we learned how to perform first aid, such as how to dress a sucking chest wound, place a splint on a broken bone, how to dress a head wound, and then how to use a tourniquet and the best place to place it to get the bleeding stop. We then we had to learn how to call for a Medevac on the radio.

* * * *

"Time was slowly moving now, and I would love a good cup of coffee right now."

* * * * *

We were at the hand grenade range. Here we learned how to use a hand grenade and how to throw one. Once the drill instructors saw we had a good understanding on how to use a grenade, they took us out to this range that they had set up for us to train on. Once we were done with the grenade training, we moved on to the M18A1 Claymore Mine training. Here they taught us how to use one and how to set it up. Once they had shown us how to set one up, we had to disarm it and place it back in the bandolier. We had to show them what we had learn that day before moving on to the minefield training. Here they showed us how to find mines that have been planted by the enemy. By the time we were done with this training, it' was supper.

The next day before breakfast, we went out and did some more hard exercises training.

* * * * *

"John, I just thought I was in good shape until then."

* * * * *

Once we were done with breakfast, we went out to the training area to provide simulated fire cover for each other while we moved from one fighting position to another. We had to get as close as we could to this machine gun that they had set up for us to take out with a hand grenade.

* * * * *

"Son, did you all use any live fire at any time during your training?"

"John, the only two times we used any live fire was when we qualified with our weapon. The drill instructors used live fire once when we had to learn how to low crawl moving under concertina wire. We also learned how to do this on our back as well as on our stomach.

"Now, John, about midway through our training, we got these cadets from West Point. No, John, at the time, we didn't know what a cadet was. Our drill sergeant had us on break. Well, one of these cadets walked up and asked why we didn't come to parade rest when he walked up. We answered him with we didn't know that we were supposed to, and we didn't know what his rank was. He then explained to us what his rank was as he put us in the front leaning rest opposition. 'Just what is a cadet? A cadet officer is like unto a second lieutenant.'

* * * * *

The next day, we got to make our one phone call home for the first time since we've been in training. The drill sergeant marched us up to the top of the hill to where the payphones were. We were standing in line at the phones, and one of the other privates asked if he could get a dip of smokeless tobacco. Well, as I gave it to him, up walked his drill sergeant. He told me and two others that we had to leave the phone booths just because his private asked for a dip from me. He also said we were to tell our drill sergeant why we were not allowed to use the phones. So we went back and let our drill sergeant know what was going on, and he began to laugh and said, "Oh really? Okay, you all can go over to the phones at the chow hall and use them." He gave us extra duty that night. Once we were done with KP…

* * * * *

"Wait now, son, what does KP stand for?"
"KP duty is Kitchen Police working under the kitchen staff. Is there anything else you would like to know before I continue with my story?"
"No, son, I guess not."

* * * * *

Now as I was about to say, we had primitive guard. Man, I tell you, a thunderstorm came that night like no one's business. We were out in it for about four hours, it seemed. The only other time I had seen it rain like this was the night we were out conducting field exercise. We had bed down for the night, and while we were asleep, there came up this real bad thunderstorm with lightning popping all around us. Our drill sergeants got us up in the middle of the night to take down our tents. They said it was very unsafe for us to stay out here with the lightning popping all around us. We needed to get back to the barracks. So one of the drill sergeants called back to home station for a bus to come pick us up. We were back to the barracks and I was told that I had fireguard duty.

One of the duties of being a fireguard was to make sure that everyone's footlocker and wall locker were secured with locks. We just got back from out of the woods, and everyone just threw their field gear either in the wall locker and the footlocker, and they didn't put their locks back on. I was downstairs in the latrine when I heard someone knocking on the door. I went to see who it could be. It was a female major and a captain who said, "We are here to do an inspection of you barracks." The other fireguard went to get our drill sergeant. As we are waiting on the drill sergeant, I was thinking, "Now why are we having an inspection at this time of night?" Well, we came to find out it was an inspection of the sensitive items.

The next morning, we went down to the sandpit for some combative training. I didn't know which of the two I hated the most, having sand in my pants or sawdust. To be completely honest, I didn't rightly care for either one of them being in my pants. Once we were done with our training, they sent us up the hill. As I make my way up the hill, I accidentally bumped into one of the drill instructors; she dropped me right there in my tracks. She said, "You ate up, private. Drop and give me ten push-ups for bumping into me." We were marching back to the barracks for lunch, and the drill sergeant was calling cadence. They said that in the army, the food was mighty fine, then a chicken jumped off the table and started marching in time. I was thinking, "Well, it might be if they would have cooked that chicken before putting it on the table." But before we could go to lunch that particular day, we had to practice drill and ceremony, for graduation day was getting closer.

After lunch, we went back out to the training area for more high-speed training. Here, we'll be training on how to use an MK19 grenade launcher. We started the class out by them telling us one of the most important things in using the MK 19 was to make sure that the back-blast area was all clear. For the back blast was just as dangerous as the front was. After a day with learning how to use the MK 19, we went back for PT. Well, this time, our drill sergeant was on the platform, conducting the exercises. He called out for our first exercise. We started with the push-up front leaning rest position move, and he fell off the podium face first.

* * * * *

"John, why are you laughing? Did I say something funny?"

"No, son, you didn't. I was just thinking back when I dropped a piece of ice down Mary's pants at school."

"John, why would you do something like that?"

"Son, she looked hot in those tight-fitting jeans she had on that day. All I was trying to do was cool her down, hmm."

"John, the way you are sounding, I might need to be the one who put the ice down your pants."

"Now why are you laughing, Son?"

"John, you said 'tight-fitting jeans.' It reminded me of this song by Conway Twitty. It's about this woman who married a millionaire, but her dream was to be just a good ole boy's girl."

"Ms. Mary, did you get back at him?"

"Son, she ran and told the teacher about what I did. The teacher confronted me about what I've done and told me that was very mean of me, and I should apologize to her. I told her I was sorry even though it was funny at the time. To be honest, I would not have liked it if she had done it to me."

"Okay, John. What would you say we take a coffee break?"

"Hey, sounds like a plan to me. What about you, my love?"

"I'm down with that. My fingers could use a break from all this writing."

"Well, Ms. Mary, after reading back over what you have written thus far, how does it sound to you?"

"Son, to be completely honest, I don't think it's going to make the bestseller list. But there is very little I know about what people like to read. I have seen some stranger things happen with books that I've found to be not all that interesting."

"Ms. Mary, I'm okay with that because I'm not trying to make the bestseller list. I'm just telling my story."

"Son, I'm glad you feel that way because I wouldn't want to see you get your hopes up and it doesn't sell at all. Now are you ready to get started again?"

"No ma'am. I think I'm going to take a walk down to the ocean just to clear my mind. I might just go on over to the coffee shop and see Ms. Sue. I'll see if she would like to join me for a walk on the beach."

"Son, that sounds like a great idea. You need to get out more. Now are you going to take your notebook and pencil with you?"

"Yes, ma'am, just in case there's something that might be of interest to write down."

"John, before I head out to the beach, can I borrow your eight-track cassette player? I found these old cassettes from years ago. Man, they take me back years in time. John, you know they remind me of a time when our stepdad took us kids one year to this watermelon festival up in Smith County that they were hosting there. They grew some of the best red and yellow meter around back in those days."

"Son, just what did they do in this festival in Smith County?"

"Well, John, they had a watermelon-eating contest as well and seed-spitting contest."

"Son, I know you didn't just say a seed-spitting contest."

"Yes, sir. A seed-spitting contest is to see who could get the seeds to go the farthest. They even had people there who could impersonate Elvis Presley. One of my favorite song of his is "Love Me Tender." I used to listen to him along with Kenny Rogers, Dolly Parton, and George Jones with Tammy Wynette all the time. They are just a few of my favorite singers when I was growing up."

"Sure, son. I don't mind. Just don't let any sand get in to it. Oh wait, son. You might want to check the batteries. It may need some new ones. It's been some time since I used it."

"Do you have any new ones?"

"Yes, they are in the desk drawer. Do you need me to put them in for you?"

"No, sir. I can put them in myself, thank you."

"Hey, I was just asking. No need to get all bent out of shape."

"Do what, John?"

"Oh, it's nothing, son. I know your intellect is not that great. Just go on down to the ocean and listen to your songs and relax."

"Here, son, you might need this sunscreen lotion while you're at the beach."

"Thank you, Ms. Mary. I'll see you two later tonight for dinner."

"John, I pray that I didn't hurt his feelings by saying what I did about his so-called book."

"Oh now, Mother, I don't think that you did. You were just being honest. Besides, if he can't handle the truth, he needs to grow up. Now, Mary, will you fix me something to eat?"

"John, would a lamb chop sandwich and chips do for now? It's only an hour until supper."

"Yes, ma'am, that will be fine. Thank you, baby. Baby, just what are you fixing for supper?"

"Sweetie, I'm preparing you a dinner unlike any you have had in a long time—venison steak smothered in brown gravy with mushrooms, red and green bell peppers, red onions and okra in the peas, and green fried tomatoes just the way you like them. I'll add along a mixture of turnips and mustard greens, broccoli with cauliflower smothered in that creamy homemade goat cheese that you love so much, and cornbread. To wash it all down will be a nice cold glass of sweet lemon iced tea. Then for dessert, my favorite, an upside-down pineapple cake with homemade vanilla ice cream."

"Hmm, now baby, that sounds great. Just hold off with that sandwich. I don't want to spoil my appetite."

"Oh, you like that menu, huh?"

"Well, yes. Who in their right mind wouldn't?"

"John, I just hope Son will like it as well."

"Baby, there is no need for you to worry about anybody else liking your cooking other than me, okay?"

"Oh, by the way, John, I hope you don't mind. I have asked my daughter to join us for dinner tonight."

"Mary, I don't mind at all. Maybe Son and she will hit it off pretty good."

"John, I don't think he is her type. But who knows?"

UNWANTED SWIM
IN THE POND

As I sat here listening to the waves of ocean as they came in and went back, I remembered a time when my brother and I went to visit one of our friends who invited us to go fishing. We went in this boat and made our way out to the middle of the pond. These crazy boy went and flipped the boat over. They liked to have grounded me before we got the boat flipped back over. They thought theywould teach me how to swim, you see, but I showed them it didn't work, so the joke was on them, ha ha.

Their father was clearing some land off to put some cows. So we asked our mother if we could stay and help them in cleaning up. She said that we could if it was okay with their mother. So they went and asked their mother if we could stay the night with them. Well, that night, we camped in the back of the pastor where we had this brush piled up to be burned as our campfire. As I looked back on those days, I got to say they were some of the best times of my life. We stayed out that night until about two in the morning before we decided it was just too cold to stay any longer.

Just like now, the sun has begun to set once again over this great big blue ocean to close out another beautiful day in which our God has so blessed us with. As I made my way back to the shop, oh, how the memories of my childhood came rushing back into remembrance, for there were so many them that I don't even know where to begin writing any of them down for you. Here was one I could start with.

It was my first year at Glade Elementary School. We were out for recess playing under the pine trees, when one of the other boys and myself got into a fight over this young lady. He busted my nose. One might say he got the best of me that time, but hey, I got the girl. And to me, that was all that mattered. There was this one night when I was at this football game with Clara and some other friends. We were jumping from off the steps to see who could jump the farthest when one of my friends jumped and broke her leg. I felt so sad for her that night. I knew firsthand what a broken bone felt like; I had both arms broken at the same time.

As I looked back to that day over some odd years ago, I got to say she was just one of the many beautiful wildflowers at Clara's school that year. Well, time passed in years. We were out playing basketball on the playground and I had the ball. I was going in to take this layup shot, and as I did, someone clipped my feet out from under me. I hit the ground face first, knocking me out cold. When I came to, I found myself lying on the ground with the other boys and girls standing around me. I had no idea what just happened to me; all I knew was that I had this headache unlike any other that I have ever had before. I went back to the classroom. The teacher asked, "Are you all right, Son?"

I replied, "No, ma'am. My head is hurting from going face first to the ground."

"Son, what did she say?"

"She sent me to the office; the secretary asked me what was wrong. I told her that I got a headache; she checked my temperature and said that was all she could do then sent me back to class."

* * * * *

I'm going to stop here for now for my head is killing me and get some rest. You look like you need to get your beauty sleep as well, ha ha. Good night, may you rest in the comfort of knowing God's love for you will forevermore be held within the hearts of those who love you. Farewell, my friend. Until we meet again tomorrow. That's if God sees fit to bless us to do so.

AN AFTERNOON WITH SUE AND MARIANNE

"Afternoon, Marianne. How have you been since the last time I've seen you?"

"Well, look who decided to stop by for a visit, our old friend Stash. Hey, Sue, Stash is here."

"Hello, Sue, it's nice to see you today. How have you been?"

"I'm doing okay, thanks for asking. Can I get you a cup of coffee?"

"Sure, why not. Thank you. I'm thinking now what's up with these two this afternoon."

"Stash, how is your book doing?"

"Which one, Marianne? The one I'm working on now or the one that is out now?"

"The one you have out now on Amazon."

"I don't know, Marianne. I haven't had time to check lately. I've been working on this other project that I got going on. Sue, how are things going for you?"

"Well, things are looking a lot better. My lawyer said my divorce should be final within the next week. We are now waiting for the judge to get back from his vacation in the Bahamas to sign it."

"It must be nice to take a vacation to the Bahamas. I heard it's very nice there this time of the year."

"Stash, that is something I will never know because I don't see myself of ever having that kind of money working here."

"Sue, who's saying that you got to work here for the rest of your life?"

"Oh, only me, Stash, for I don't have any other place to go."

"Sue, if you don't ever try to find a better place to work, you won't find the happiness that you so greatly deserve."

"Yeah, right, Stash. You don't know just how hard it is for a woman to find a job here in this desert town."

"Sue, if I were a betting man, I would bet with your knowledge you could become a lawyer yourself if you so choose."

"Stash, that is very kind of you to say, but I don't think being a lawyer is for me. Stash, that notebook you got there, does it have anything to do with that new project you've been working on?"

"Yes, ma'am, it does at that. Would you like to read over it and tell me what you think?"

"Sure, I'd be glad to read over it for you, that's if you have time."

"Sue, I got all the time in the world, for I have no specific place to be. Besides, I would like to use your computer to check my e-mail, if you don't mind."

"Stash, I don't have mine with me today. I can ask Marianne if you can borrow hers."

"Here you go. Stash."

"Thanks, Marianne. It's very kind of you to allow me to use your personal computer."

"Oh, Stash, it's no problem. My little brother uses it all the time to play Candy Crush and Golf Clash. Stash, have you heard anything lately on your book?"

"No, Marianne, I haven't in the past month or so. Your computer is not connecting to the internet for some reason."

"Here, let me see it. Sometimes, I must go in and reboot the hard drive after my brother's been on it."

"Stash, so far, this is good."

"Thank you, Sue."

"Stash, I find it to be fascinating the way you are mixing your childhood memories in with your military story. Has Mrs. John been helping you any?"

"Sue, she's looking over the sentence structure and for any errors in my Southern slang grammar. She's all the time correcting my grammar as I'm talking to John. Ladies, I must be going now. I told Mrs. John I'd be back in time for supper. She said we're going to have a special guest coming tonight."

"Did she say who this special guest is?"

"No, she didn't say. I'll see you two later."

"Okay, Stash, good night. And good luck with your book."

"Thanks, Sue, and thank you, Marianne, for the use of your computer."

As I walked along the ocean, I looked down and saw these fishes, so I stopped to watch them. As I was watching them, my mind slipped back into a time when my brothers, cousins, and I would go fishing. If we weren't catching any fish at Nicholson Creek, we would walk the Blackman Branch or Rita Branch trying our fishing skills. Man, how I missed those hot summer days. Life back in those days seemed to have been the happiest and carefree time in life. For back then, it seemed as if everyone had more love and respect for each other than what they do in the times wherein we are living today. As I slowly walked back to John's, I was thinking to myself all the killings of innocent lives in this past year by people who had no regard for human life. For there just seemed to be so much more hatred in this old world today than what it was back then.

As I made my way into the house, I saw a dozen of red roses sitting on the table.

"Hi, Ms. Mary, whatever you are cooking smells good."

"Thanks, son."

"Ms. Mary, your roses are beautiful. Did Mr. John do something wrong?"

"Ha ha. No, my daughter brought them for me. Tomorrow is my birthday."

"Hmm, roses for ma'am, now that reminds me of this song by Red Sovine called, 'A Red Rose for Mama.' It's about this young boy who wants to buy five roses for his mother's birthday. Wait just a minute. Did you say your daughter is here?"

"Yes, son, my daughter. I told you we were going to have a special guest over tonight. She's in the bedroom putting her things up. She and John just got here about ten minutes ago."

"Mary, how much longer will it be before we eat?"

"John, I am waiting on the cornbread. Once it's done, then we can eat. John, you could help by setting the table."

"Yes, ma'am."

"Mother, is there anything that I can help with?"

"No, Lana. Oh, by the way, Lana, this is Son, sometimes known as Stash."

"Hello, Lana." Oh man, of all times for my mind to go blank.

"Hello, Stash, it's nice to finally meet you. Mother has told me a lot about you."

I was thinking, *Oh wait, no. I'm not going to say that.* "Well, Lana, I hope it wasn't all bad."

"No, Stash, it wasn't anything like that. She just said that you wrote a book about this man being on a journey looking for his soul mate. Do you have one with you?"

"No, Lana. I don't currently have one."

"Where can I find one of your books?"

"Ms. Lana, the last time I've checked, it's on Amazon or Barnes & Noble. They have it in all three formats and editions."

"Stash, when I get back home, I'll look it up on my Kindle. I would like to read it.

"Hey, John, it's time to eat. Lana, you can sit here by Stash."

"Oh, Mother, Stash might not want to sit by me."

"Ms. Lana, I don't really mind if you do. It would be my honor."

"Mary, you've once again gone and outdone yourself with dinner."

"Ms. Mary, I'm going to agree with John. This is one of the best home-cooked meals I've had since…well…let's just say in a long time."

"Thank you, both. Lana, did your brothers say what time they're coming over tomorrow?"

"No, Mother. I only got to talk with Lawrence, and he didn't say anything about what time he and Jan, that old stuck-up wife of his, would head this way."

"Now, Lana, baby, you know that's no way to speak of your sister-in-law. She can't help that she thinks she's better than everyone else just because she was born with a silver spoon in her mouth.

"What's wrong, Son? Are you okay?"

"No, ma'am. My heart feels as if it's going to beat right through my chest."

"Lana, you are a registered nurse, check his blood pressure."

"Mother, I can't get a reading of his blood pressure. His heart is beating way too fast. Son, are you having shortness of breath, any dizziness or headache?"

"Well, I do have a headache, and I do feel a little dizzy, but no shortness of breath."

"Have you ever experienced this before?"

"Yes, ma'am. I have once before."

"What were you doing at the time that it happened?"

"I was headed home from my nephew's homecoming football game when this other vehicle had at one point left the road and hit someone's driveway, causing him to lose control of his vehicle, throwing him back out into the highway right in front of me. I'm guessing from the impact of the airbag hitting me in the chest caused it to run away."

"Son, were you in the same truck that you and your brother were in when it was airborne?"

"No, John, it was not the same truck. Although, that truck has a whole different story behind itself. If I live long enough, I will tell you a few of them."

"Oh, son, we got time. You aren't going to die just yet. You can tell me now."

"No, John, he can't right now. Son, either you've had a heart attack or you are in the process of having one. John, we need to take him to the hospital. They can do an ECG or an EKG on him. His heart has gone into SVT."

"Wait now, Lana. Just what is SVT? Is that something serious?"

"Son, just get in the vehicle, okay? I will explain it on the way to the hospital. John, we need to go now."

"Lana, you were going to tell me what SVT is."

"Son, it's short for supraventricular tachycardia, which is a rapid heart rate above hundred beats per minute. It is caused by electrical impulses that originate above the heart's ventricles."

"So is that why my heart has an abnormal rhythm?"

"Yes, son."

"Hmm, and here I was thinking it was caused by me sitting by a super-hot, gorgeous woman the whole time."

"Son, I got to say you do have a vivid imagination."

"Well, thank you, Lana. I can assure you that's not all I have."

"Hey, I need a wheelchair out here. I have someone who is possibly having a heart attack."

"What's the problem out here?"

"Doctor, he says he is experiencing SVT."

"Hmm, now let me see here. What do we need to do first?"

"Son, just to let you know, it's been sometime since I've treated someone who is experiencing SVT. But don't worry yourself. Son, you are in good hands. I'm going to see that you get the best treatment that your money can buy."

I was thinking, "Now this treatment will not go very far on the amount of money that I have."

"Son, the first thing we need to do is get you hooked up to the electrocardiogram (ECG) so I can see just what your heart is doing."

"Doc, just what is electrocardiogram?"

"Son, they are electrodes placed on the skin of your chest and connected in a specific order to a machine that when turned on, would measure and record the electrical activity of your heart."

"Now, doc, I don't see any need of doing all of that. I can tell you what it's doing—it's beating very fast."

"Okay now, son, you need to just listen to me for once. Lie back and relax, and let me do my job."

Hmm, when he said relax, it got me thinking back to this time when I had to go to the dentist to have a crown replaced. The next thing I realized, I was in this room, and someone was trying to stick me in the army with what felt like a big vampire needle to draw blood.

"Now, son, I know you are not telling me you're scared of needles."

"No, John, I'm not scared of needles. I just don't like getting stuck with them."

"Mr. John, I need you to stand back or wait outside. We will take care of him, okay?"

"Well, okay, doc."

"Son, I'm going to be right over here if you need anything."

"John, now that you mention it, I would like a cup of coffee."

"No, son, you cannot have a cup of coffee right now with your heart in SVT. Nurse, you need to get him hooked to the ECG."

"Yes, doctor."

"Son take off your…hmm."

"Nurse, is there something wrong?"

"Ah…no, son. There is nothing wrong. It's just that I've never seen such a nice-looking chest such as yours before."

"Oh, really, you don't say. Hmm, then if you don't mind me saying, you have the most beautiful eyes I've seen in quite some time. As I look into your eyes, they remind me of a song by Conway Twitty, 'Those Eyes,' and another one of my favorite song of his, 'I Want to Know You.'"

"Son, just who is Conway Twitty?"

"Oh, Conway is just one of the most beloved country singers of all time. From 1971 to 1976, Harold Lloyd Jenkins received a string of Country Music Association awards for duets with Loretta Lynn. He died back in 1993 on June 5."

"Who is Harold Lloyd Jenkins you are talking about now?"

"Harold is Conway Twitty. Conway Twitty was just his stage name."

"Son, I'm going to inject a medication into your IV drip. It will help slow your heart rate down."

"Okay, do what every you got to do."

"Hmm, son, I've never seen this medication take this long to work."

"Did I just get kicked in the chest by a mule? Because that hurt."

"No, son. That's just the medication. Now in the meantime, just lay back and try to relax. I'm going to check on your blood work."

"Son, your blood work shows that everything is normal. It could have been that your electrolytes could have gotten out of balance, causing your heart to go into SVT. You do know that humans need electrolytes to survive? For a healthy function of the heart as well as the body,, we must have a balance of different electrolytes interacting with each other throughout the cells in the tissues, nerves, and muscles. Now I'm going to set you up an appointment with a heart specialist. He can do a more in- depth study of your heart and tell you what is going on with your heart. This could take up to a week are two. In the meantime, I'm going to prescribe you this medication. It will help regulate your heart rate."

"Okay, doc. I'm looking forward to getting to the bottom of this SVT, since you think it wasn't caused by me sitting by a beautiful lady."

"You are welcome, son, and good luck."

"Son, while you are waiting on the nurse to get the discharge papers done, I'll go bring the truck around."

"Good, because I'm ready to go home."

"Son, here are your discharge papers and the prescription for your medication. I'll be back with a wheelchair to take you out to your car."

"Okay, thank you, ma'am."

"John, can we stop by the pharmacy so I can get this medication?"

"Yeah, I guess so. That's if you don't mind getting me a cold drink."

"Son, why are you so quiet tonight?"

"Mrs. John, after they slowed my heart rate down, my brain activity is racing."

"Stash, you know that your brain controls everything from your heart rate to your mood. Your brain contains billions of nerve cells that are arranged in such a pattern that coordinate your thought, emotion, as well as your behavior, movement, and sensation. With all the parts of the brain working together, each part is responsible for a specific function of the body. Stash, do you also know that your body has two nervous systems? One is called the central nervous system (CNS), and the other is the peripheral nervous system. It's based on their location in the body. The CNS includes the nerves in your brain and spinal cord."

"Wait now, Ms. Lana. All this information is good to know, but I need to call it a night, okay?"

"Okay, Stash. Good night. Hope you sleep well."

"Thank you, ma'am, and same to you as well. Mr. and Mrs. John, good night."

"Good night, son. See you in the morning."

* * * * *

Before I lay myself down to sleep tonight, let's investigate the living word of God. I may have already shared these words earlier with you, but with everything that is going on in my life right now; I'm feeling the need to read them once again.

> He giveth power to the faint; and to them that have no might he increaseth strength. Even the youths shall faint and be weary, and the young men shall utterly fall: But they that wait upon the Lord shall renew their strength; they shall mount up with wings as eagles; they shall run, and not be weary; and they shall walk, and not faint. (Isa. 40:29–31).

Now let me see if I can recall this old prayer I've learned as a young boy.

> Now I lay myself down to sleep, if I should die before I awake, I pray the Lord my soul to keep forevermore. Thank you, O Lord thy God for loving us. Good night.

THE WEEK BEFORE CHRISTMAS

"GOOD MORNING, MRS. JOHN. HAPPY birthday. May God's blessings be upon you throughout your new year."

Good morning to you also, son, and thank you for the birthday wishes. Son, would you like a nice cup of coffee to start your day?"

"Yes, I would, thank you. Ms. Mary, you know in a week, we'll be celebrating the birth of our Lord Jesus Christ."

Yes, son, I know. It's hard to believe that another year has also come and gone. It seems only yesterday that Lana, Lawrence, and Joe were still little children. We would all gather on Christmas Eve night around the tree, and Joe Sr., their farther, would read to them the story about how the birth of Jesus came about from the book of Luke 1:26–35 (KJV).

> And in the sixth month the angel Gabriel was sent from God unto a city of Galilee, named Nazareth. To a virgin espoused to a man whose name was Joseph, of the house of David; and the virgin's name was Mary. And angel came in unto her, and said, Hail, thou that art highly favoured, the Lord is with thee: blessed art thou among women. And when she saw him, she was troubled at his saying, and cast in her

mind what manner of salutation this should be. And the angel said unto her, Fear not Mary: for thou hast found favour with God. And, behold, thou shalt conceive in thy womb, and bring forth a son, and shalt call his name JESUS. He shall be great and shall be called the Son of the Highest: and the Lord God shall give unto him the throne of his father David: And he shall reign over the house of Jacob forever; and of the kingdom there shall be no end. Then said Mary unto the angel, How shall this be, seeing I know not a man? And the angel answered and said unto her, The Holy Ghost shall come upon thee, and the power of the Highest shall over-shadow thee: therefore, also that holy thing which shall be born of thee shall be called the Son of God.

"Ms. Mary, you know this is the most amazing time of the year."

"Oh, you don't say."

"Yes, ma'am. I do say, for it is a time that born-again Christians celebrate that God gave his only begotten Son so that whosoever believes upon him shall have everlasting life in thy Father's kingdom."

"Son, you are right about God giving his Son as a Redeemer for our sins, but there is more to this than just believing upon his name."

"Good morning, Mother, and you also, Stash. Happy birthday, Mom. I love you."

"Thank you, Lana. I love you too. What would you like for breakfast?"

"Mom, I'm good with whatever everyone else is having. What were y'all talking about when I walked in?"

"I was telling Son how your dad would read to you kids how the birth of Jesus came about, the night before Christmas."

"Oh, Mom, those are some of the best memories that I have of Dad. He would also read on Christmas morning from the book of Matthew how the three wise men came from Jerusalem, bearing gifts, before he would let us open our gifts."

"Lana, I'm surprised you remember him doing that for it was such a long time ago."

"Mom, I remember it as if it was last night. He would start in Matthew 2:9–12 (KJV)":

> When they had heard the king, they departed; and, lo, the star, which they saw in the east, went before them, till it came and stood over where the young child was. When they saw the star, they rejoiced with exceeding great joy. And when they were come into the house, they saw the young child with Mary his mother, and fell, and worshipped him: and when they had opened their treasures, they presented unto him gifts; gold, and frankincense, and myrrh. And being warned of God in a dream that they should not return to Herod, they departed into their own country another way.

MY ADVENTURES CONTINUE WITH THE 624TH QM

"John, how are you?"

"I'm great, thanks for asking. Now where is my cup of coffee?"

"John, here's your coffee. Would you like me to fix you something to eat?"

"Yes, ma'am, if you don't mind. I would love to have four of your blueberry waffles."

"Son, what do you have planned for your day?"

"John, I'm going to spend the day with Sue and Marianne down at the beach. We are going to work on my book."

"Son, Mary was hoping you would spend the day with us. She wants you to meet her family."

"John, I would love to meet her family, but I need to work on my book."

"Well, son, I was under the impression that you wanted me and Ms. Mary to help you."

"John, it's not that I don't appreciate your help or anything. It's just that you are always interrupting me with questions."

"Well, excuse me, son. I didn't know that by me asking a question every now and then was a problem."

"John, your questions do have ways of interrupting my train of thoughts."

"Well, just go and tell your story to Sue and Marianne and see if it turns out as good as if Mary and I had helped you."

"John, that is just what I'm going to do. See you later."

* * * * *

"Marianne, where's Sue? I was hoping you two would be ready to go down to the beach and get started working on my book."

"Oh, Stash, just hold your horses. We'll be ready in about five minutes."

"Ladies, before we get started, I would like to ask if you would please hold any questions until the end."

"Okay, sure, Stash."

"It was after graduating from basic training at Ft. Jackson. I returned home before continuing to Ft. Lee for my MOS training. Once I got to Ft. Lee for my MOS training, I became more familiar with the equipment that I would be working with back at my home unit. The senior instructor, whose name was Workman, believed me when I said he lived up to his name very well. He worked us like there was no tomorrow in sight. We laid out fuel bags and built the burns around them by our own hands, using only shovels, wheelbarrow, and picks, of course. Once the burns were to standards, we laid out the hose line and gate valves for hookup. But before this took place, we spent hours in the classroom learning how this was done. We then moved on to the next portions of our training, which consisted of transferring the fuel from railcars to fuel tanks for storage. Once in storage, we would learn how to pull samples of the fuel and check for contamination. Then came the different types of vehicles that would be used in handling the fuel. My favorite vehicle to operate was once known as the 49th Charlie."

"Stash, you don't say."

"Now, Marianne, the 49th Charlie was the workhorse of its time, until the HEMTT fueler came along, pushing it out. Once my training at Ft. Lee on how to handle fuel and how to operate the equipment was completed, I was released back to my home unit as a qualified fuel handler."

"So you say."

"John, I heard that. And just to let you know, our instructors made sure you knew your job in handing fuel and all the equipment before letting you graduate from AIT. Mogas, JP8, and diesel fuel can kill you in an instant if not correctly handled. I'm thinking it was my second drill back that my platoon sergeant put me in for the soldier of the month awards. I had to go before the first sergeant and the company commander, who would ask me a series of questions to see if I qualified for this award. I remember this one question the commander asked on how I felt about my appearance as a soldier, not knowing the correct way to answer."

"Stash, how did you answer him?"

"John, I replied, 'Sir, there's always room for improvement.' He looked me in the eyes. I was thinking maybe that wasn't the answer he wanted to hear.

"He said, 'So you're telling me that we all can make improvements to our appearance? Good answer.

"Moving on in time to my first summer camp with the unit at Camp Shelby. We were getting our area of operations set up when this two-star general showed up for a visit. The commander asked if I would show him around and explain what we were doing. I was thinking, 'Now of all people, you just had to go and ask me, the newest member of the unit. I've never met a two-star general before in person.' As we were walking around the area of operation, he would ask me some questions like how I liked being in the 624th QM, and how long have I been with the unit. Did I have any plans of making a career of being in the National Guard? My answer to his question was, 'Sir, currently, I don't know just what I'm going to do. This is my first summer camp with the unit, and I have five more years to go. Then, I will have a better idea as what I will do.' We made our way back to where we had started. We took a picture or two, and I once again gave him the greeting of the day and returned to work. It was 1986, my first of many summer camps with the unit at Camp Shelby.

"The summer of 1987, we went back to Camp Shelby for another training event, but at a different location. We arrived at our new location right at dark. We hadn't had time to set up a good perimeter defense around our compound. The OP force snuck in later that night and took our cooking pots and pans. We could hear the rattling of the pots and pans as they ran thought the woods. I just thought it was the cooks setting up for the morning chow. That was when I heard the cooks yell out, 'Stop! Stop them. They are taking our pots and pans.' I just laid back down in my cart, pulling my sleeping bag over my head, thinking to myself, 'I'm not going to chase after them at eleven o'clock at night in these woods. You can just forget that. They can have those pots and pans. I'm going back to sleep.' Now thirty plus years later, I'm sharing with you some of my fondest memories of my time served with the Guard.

"Time continued to move forward in years. In 1989, George H. W. Bush was elected as the president. During his time in office, we became involved with liberating Kuwait from the invasion of Iraq, which was controlled by Saddam Hussein. This began to take place in August 1990. I was only married for two months when I received the call at 11:00 p.m. on the November 11 that we were to report to the unit in preparation for mobilization. The 624 QM would receive their mob orders on November 17, 1990, to report to Ft. Benning, Georgia, on November 20 for training for combat in support of Operation Desert Shield, Desert Storm. This would become one of the most emotional times ever in the history of the unit and its surrounding family's communities. There were only a few of the unit members that had ever served in combat. They served was during the Vietnam conflict.

"As the days continued to draw closer, the unit packed up their remaining equipment in preparation for their departure to Ft. Benning. On the day of our departure, the roadway was lined with family and friends to show their support. There was not a dry eye to be found on the grounds of that place—no, not a one, I say.

"I'm sorry, I'm going to have step away for a minute. I'm getting all choked up just thinking back to those times. Okay, let me try this again.

"We gave our loved ones one last hug and kiss before loading the buses and the military vehicles. As we made our way onto Highway 63, being led by the local law enforcement. You know something, our law enforcement, they themselves are some of the nicest people you'd ever meet, and my hat goes off to you men and women, for I know you yourself face the danger of war every day. We moved out slowly until the entire convoy was on the road en route bound for Georgia. As the convoy slowly made its way through our hometown of Waynesboro, to our surprise, there were people of all ages standing by the side of the road waving the American flag high; and some were holding up signs that said, 'We love y'all.' I was in the passenger seat trying my best once again to hold back the tears. But I couldn't.

"That day, they flowed down my cheeks like a small stream flowing into a river as we passed them by. It was like this all the way to Quitman and up through Meridian and some over into Alabama. The transportation unit from Quitman, Mississippi, and the unit from Lucedale had also received their mob orders in support of the conflict with the Iraqi Army. I was thinking, 'I'm going to become a casualty of war before we even get there due to dehydration with all these tears.'

"I know this is very unlikely, unless you haven't been drinking enough fluid. That night, we had to make a refuel stopover in a small town in Alabama before continuing to Ft. Benning. On the morning of our arrival, they placed us at Churchill in these old World War II barracks. During our time at Ft. Benning, we received medical treatment and all shots that were needed to bring our medical and dental records up-to-date. I remember this one shot that they gave me in the hip. Man, it hurt for days on end. Once done with the medical update, we trained on our operations on what would be done in support of this conflict with Saddam Hussein's army. We got to go home one last time for Thanksgiving before leaving for the Middle East. Once we arrived in the country on January 2, 1991, the pilot came over the intercom saying, 'Welcome to Saudi Arabia. Your current temperature outside is a comfortable 75 degrees.' So our commander said we could roll up our sleeves. But when the door opened and the first person stepped to the door, their sleeves came down and the field jackets came out. I was thinking his thermometer was broken for it felt more like 40 degrees instead of 75. We unloaded our equipment and reloaded it onto the baggage trucks to go to the Port near Dhahran.

"On the way to the port, the bus driver stopped and got off the bus right in the middle of the street and used the restroom right beside the bus. We all looked at each other like, 'What is going on here?' He got back on the bus and we continued for what seemed like another four hours. We stayed in this large warehouse beside the port with around nine hundred or more soldiers for about two weeks. We came under the command of the Second COS-COM.

"While in country, I learned that there was a MASH Unit named 4077, and my first time ever seeing green scrambled eggs. We were standing in line for breakfast one morning and I was talking with this medical officer, who told me that he was with the MASH Unit 4077. Before I could ask, he blurted out, 'No, we don't have a Major Hot Lips Houlihan, but I've seen green scrambled eggs before. I don't recommend we eat them.' We had to convert back to eating MRE three times a day until they got new cooks to prepare our food. My favorite was the frankfurters with cheese and crackers.

"Whoops! Sorry, got to go here. The restrooms consisted of plywood place around 55-gallon drums cut in half with plywood place over them and holes to serve as seats. One night, I had to go to the outhouse, and on my way there, I saw a group of people headed my way. It was the officers, so I gave the greetings of the day with a salute. She was a female warrant officer whom I was under the impression was with the group. She pulled me off to the side and began to chew me out for not giving her a salute as well.

"That very night, the sirens began going off, signifying that we were under attack from the Iraqi army. We've been told if the sirens were to go off, we were to find cover and get into our MOPP Four because of the threat from chemical weapons being used by the Iraqi army. That very same night, we had a soldier who panicked and tried to put the bottom of his or her MOPP (chemical suit) on for the top. No, it wasn't me this time. I was only asked to share only the story with you and not to reveal the name.

"Now the showers were built in the same fashion. They have water tanks placed on top of the structure to supply the water. The only way we could heat the water was with submergible heaters. Once the unit had received most of its equipment, we went to the fuel point with the tanker to pick up fuel for the remaining vehicles. On our way, we heard the sirens once again going off. We looked and saw a patriot missile going over. I'm not 100 percent sure if this was around the same time that the scud missile killed the twenty-seven American soldiers and wounding ninety-eight others; or if this happened after we had left the port. We got orders to relocate to this camp called Log Base Nelligan, which would later become known to the occupants as Log Base Mason Dixon. Along the route to Log Base Nelligan, we would have to cross the Kuwaiti-Iraqi border. Before proceeding forward across the border, we stopped and pulled security. There were blown up Iraqi tanks and trucks as far as you could see along the road before continuing our move to Log Base Nelligan. It began to rain as it was now. I guess you could say we got our shower for that night or for the week. We arrived there around midnight and had to use the lights from our vehicles to get the fuel farm set up, which consisted of two 50 kg bags of mogas, and two 500 gal drums of mogas; eight 50 kg bags of diesel, and one 50 kg bags of JP-8, four 500 gal drums of JP-8, which is known as a FARP site for refueling helicopters. The FARP site itself had to be set up a great distance from the rest of the operations because of the helicopters having to set down for refueling."

"Before we could get everything set in place to begin to receive fuel, we had fuel tanks to come in. We had to do a tanker-to-tanker transfer to keep the flow of fuel moving to the warfighters. We were fighting the elements of the desert and its high winds; it was picking the bags from off the ground and us with it. It took all that we could do in keeping the bags in place until we got fuel into them. We worked in shifts in doing this, and at the end of my shift, I went to sleep on the back of the 2.5 ton cargo truck. When I woke up from my deep sleep that morning, I was in total shock because the place had been transformed in a way that I didn't recognize. There for a second, when I first looked around, I thought I had been taken by the Iraqi army. They had set up tents all around the compound. The engineers had come in and built a berm around the perimeter of our compound and around the fuel bags. They had also dug a burn pit for the waste on the outside of the compound. For days on, we would work on improving our living conditions. We built the showers and toilets like unto the ones that was back at the port. We dug foxholes and camouflaged them with netting and sandbags. The foxhole was used for pulling perimeter guard for the compound. It seemed like every morning we were getting up at four o'clock.

"As time continued, we had put up concertina wire on the perimeter berm to help increase the security for the compound. Unlike the army today, we had to go old school, meaning we had to make do with what we had at the time. We didn't have any indoor plumbing with running hot water to take a shower or do our laundry with. We used ten-gallon buckets to do laundry in and hung them on a line to dry from the desert heat, which didn't take long. If you didn't get this done before midafternoon, you would be washing them again because of the sandstorm. They came daily there along with the sand/blow flies. The sand was like fine powder. It would stick to wet clothes, making them as stiff as cardboard. We were on our lunch break one day when we saw this sandstorm headed in our direction; it seemed to be turning the skies into a dark-red color. The high winds were sweeping across the dry desert ground, picking up its sand as it moved swiftly across the open desert. You could see this several miles away. I remember this well, for I had just walked back into our tent when it hit camp. The sides of the tent flapped from the high winds, causing some of the poles to fall; one liked to hit me. Once the storm had passed, we went out, and we would find that the cook's tent had been ripped in half from the high winds. Until the cooks could get their new tent put up, and the MKT back in operation, our meals would be MREs three times a day for the next four days."

"Stash, if you don't mind, I'm in need of a restroom break."

"Sure, Marianne, why not. I need to go myself."

"Now, Stash, before we get started, can I ask if you saw any dead people during your time there?"

"Well, Marianne, actually, I can't say that I did or not, other than the ones that were already in body bags on this helicopter that came in for refuel one afternoon. My brother was running the site at this time. I had walked out there to ask him something, when I saw these black bags lying on the floor of the chopper. I asked what those are. The pilot answered, "Oh, those are bodies." I did a hasty 180, forgetting what I had walked out there for. Now, Marianne, that is as close as I ever came to seeing any dead people."

"This all took place during the air campaign, which started on January 17 and ending on February 23 of 1991. Then came the ground invasion which only lasted for a hundred hours. Once the ground war ended and all the warfighters had returned from off the battlefield, we received orders to cease fuel operations and start preparing to return back across the border into Kuwait. Midway of the operation breakdown, our commander sent a small group of us back to start washing the equipment going to the port for the journey home. In between time of receiving and washing the equipment as it came in, we would have some down time. In passing time, we would either play ping pong, volleyball, or horseshoes.

"One late afternoon after work, a friend and I were out playing ping pong, when the darkness of the desert came upon us. Well, my friend decided to poke a hole in the ball and pour the liquid from the chem-light into the ball so that we could keep playing; it only worked for about ten minutes. We didn't have the type of Morale, Welfare, and Recreation (MWRs) or United Service Organizations (USOs) like they do today over there, for we were only there for five months. Now speaking of the USO, they did provide free calling cards from AT&T. Now AT&T have a satellite phone station set up about two or more miles from our compound. If you ever got the chance to go, you go; you couldn't just go up and walk there. Now all the different units who used the phone service had to provide personnel for security. The day came for our unit to provide phone security, so I volunteered. We had only been there for maybe three hours or so when two of our unit members showed up with orders not to let any of our people use the phones. You know the first thing came to my mind was *why*. I asked, 'What is going on?'

"The sergeant replied, 'You'll find out when you get back to the compound.'

"Our shift had ended for the day. We got back and found out that one of our friends had died from a heart attack after playing volleyball. That day in history of the 624th QM Unit will forever be remembered as the saddest day of the whole deployment. The unit couldn't return home for the funeral service.

"I'm sorry. I'm going to take a step back for a minute."

"Stash, are you going to be okay?"

"Yes, Sue. I'll be okay. It's just thinking back on those days bring back some great memories and some sad ones."

"Stash, if you need to stop here and pick back up some other time, we'd understand."

"No, Marianne. I need to get as much written today as I can.

"Now only days from returning home, the unit members held a memorial service in honor of our fallen friend."

Our brother, you've been awakened now by the One from upon High to serve in a greater calling than the one you had here among us. As you begin this new journey of yours through eternity of time, servicing alongside all our other fellow brothers and sisters who have gone on before us to serve in that much greater calling, you leave behind only your memories to be shared with your loved ones and those generations who came afterward. We who have served beside you will forevermore hold those memories in the highest regard. A brother to all, a son of two who had talked you to be the man you had become. A husband and father to all whom you loved. We of whom you leave behind must say unto you now our final farewell with only a salute. Your service to God and your free support to our country will be greatly remembered by all. We who have had the opportunity of serving with you.

As I was reading Ephesians, I came across these verses:

Wherefore he saith, "Awake thou that sleepest, and arise from the dead, and Christ shall give thee light. See then that ye walk circumspectly, not as fools, but as wise, Redeeming the time, because the days are evil. Wherefore be ye not unwise but understanding what the will of the Lord is. And be not drunk with wine, wherein is excess; but be filled with the Spirit; Speaking to yourselves in psalms and hymns and spiritual songs, singing and making melody in your heart to the Lord. Giving thanks always for all things unto God and the Father in the name of our Lord Jesus Christ." (Ephesians 5:14–20, KJV)

"Stash, I'm sorry. It's getting time for us to go work."

"Okay, Sue. Thank you both for taking the time out of your day to listen to my stories."

"Stash, you are going back with us, aren't you?"

"No, Marianne. I'm just going to hang out here for a little while longer, read my Bible, and do some more writing before heading back to John's."

"Okay, Stash. We'll see you tomorrow."

As I was sitting here, listening to the sounds of the birds as they flew over and waves of the ocean as they came and went, I was reminded of a time when some friends and I had walked down to the port of Kuwait to take some pictures of the ships as they were coming in to the port and some of the birds as they were flying over the ocean with the sun at their backs. As I looked back unto those days that now only existed in history that seemed as only yesterday, what if I had been the one who didn't come home from the war? I wonder what my last letter to my family and friends would say.

A SOLDIER'S LETTER
TO HOME

DEAR FAMILY AND FRIENDS, As I find myself beginning to prepare for this journey into combat alone with my fellow brothers and sisters in a foreign land to face a dark, evil adversary, I'm sure you know by now from watching the news we're facing an adversary who holds in his possession a deadly weapon. An evil weapon that he has used multiple times on his own people to maintain a level of control over them. For I find myself now to be in such a battle as this and may not be able to win as it continues, knowing that death can surely take anyone of us at any time. I know we all were conceived in the flesh of a woman's womb and born into the darkness of sin. I find myself asking our Lord Jesus Christ in whom you have taught me as a young child to trust in his forgiveness for our sins when we transgress against his teachings.

I know in my heart Jesus never promised me it would be an easy battle to fight alone. He only promised that if we believed in him, he would surely return one day for us. I feel within my heart that the day of my great awakening is drawing near with each breath in which I take. I know my soul has been covered by his blood, which he has so freely given to us all. For I can't even begin to imagine in my deepest pain how he must have felt that day hanging on an old rugged cross, with only three rusted nails holding him.

I leave with you only the great memories which we've made together here in this life. For I can't take them with me on my eternal journey. For those memories only exist of a time of our lives that will surely one day fade away with life itself. A journey in which we all are surely going to face in the days to come. For only our Lord thy God knows when that day is going to come. Oh, my beloved ones, do always keep yourselves ready to make that journey through eternity; and hopefully, we'll join our loved ones who have gone on before us. I can only imagine in my dreams what our lives will belike on that day of our great awakening. I'm looking forward to that day when we're able to once again embrace each other with open arms. An endless journey through eternity in which we'll be able to live without any pain or sorrow.

Only you, my Lord, know the true way to bring a heart to life that's fading fast. My family and friends, it's my hope your hearts will forevermore remember our lives we once shared here in this journey. Just one of my fondest memories that comes to mind is taking a ride on my motorcycle down the old country road to just clear my mind. Oh, how the smell of the honeysuckle, roses, and all of God's other lovely wildflowers, along with listening to the sounds of the birds chirping bring back some great childhood memories.

* * * * *

"Marianne, I hope he's going to be okay there by himself."

"Sue, you know I could tell he was getting emotional by talking about his friend passing away while servicing his country."

"Yes, Marianne. He had tears flowing down his cheeks as he was talking about that day, and that's why I said it was time for us to go because I myself started to tear up."

"Sue, so was I. I can't even begin to imagine how they must have felt being only days from returning home from their deployment, only to lose one of their friends after the war ended."

"Marianne, I know it was one of the hardest things that anyone could ever do. For the day we said farewell to my great-uncle, there wasn't a dry eye around that place."

"Sorry to hear that, Sue. How old were you when he passed?"

"Marianne, I was only about twelve years old, but I remember it as if it was only yesterday."

"Sue, I know it's hard to say goodbye to those whom we love with all our heart. When I visit my grandmother's old homestead, I can still hear their voice as they are sitting at the dinner table, discussing how rapidly things have changed over the past years. My grandmother would be telling Dad and Mom how hard her generation had to work to put food on their table and clothes on their back. Dad would say, "Well, Mom, you know that children today don't know what hard work is. Their young minds and morals have been altered by today's society into thinking that everything is to be given to them on a silver platter. The society in which they are growing up in has become so far from knowing how to think for themselves that they got to rely on others to provide for them.""

"Marianne, it's the same way when I stop by my parents' old home. I remember this one day when two of my friends had come over after school. We were playing out back in my tree house Dad had built. I stepped on this nail and it when through my shoe. Honey, I let out a scream. Dad and Mom came running out of the house to see what has happened. Dad said in his sweet voice, 'Sue your scream scared the life out of your mom.'

"'Sorry, Dad. I didn't mean to. I just stepped on a nail.'

"'We thought you fell out the playhouse and hurt yourself.'"

* * * * *

"Hi, Kim. How have things been here at the coffee shop?"

"Marianne, from the time I've got here, we have been going nonstop around the clock. I haven't even taken a break. Could you take over for me? I'm in need of a restroom break."

"Yes, Kim. I can take over for you."

"Thank you very much, Marianne."

"Marianne, you know, I can't get Stash out of my mind. I'm going to call Mrs. John to see if he has made it home."

"Okay, Sue."

"Hello."

"Yes, hello. This is Sue down at the coffee shop. May I speak with Mrs. John, please."

"Sue, this is her. How have you been?"

"Mrs. John, I'm doing well, thank you. How about yourself?"

"Sue, I'm doing great, thank you. How can I be of help to you?"

"Mrs. John, why I'm calling is to ask if Stash has made it there."

"Hold on, Sue. I think he just walked in. Hey, is that you, Stash?"

"Yes, ma'am, it's me."

"Yes, Sue. He just walked in. Would you like to speak with him?"

"No, ma'am. I just wanted to be sure he got there okay. When we left him down at the ocean, he seemed to be feeling down."

"Oh, okay. Thanks, Sue, for letting me know.

"Stash, that was Sue on the phone. She was checking on you. She said when they left you, you were feeling down about something."

"Well, Mrs. John, I'm guessing she was referring to me talking about my friend who passed away."

"Well, Stash, if you don't mind me asking, what happened to your friend?"

"Mrs. John, it's all in my notes. You and Mr. John can read over them tonight if you would like."

"Stash, you know John and I would love to read over your notes."

As we were talking, in walked someone whom I hadn't seen in many blue moons from Sunday. As she walked into the room, my eyes focused upon her and her alone. She was wearing a silky blue tank-top dress that stopped only inches above her knees, with her long silky hair draped over one shoulder, revealing only a small portion of her upper torso. Once again, the rhythm of my heart began to beat like the sound of war drums within my chest.

Oh, how her beauty alone could illuminate a room when she walked in, causing the brightest of light to dim. My eyes become drawn unto her sexy tanned legs as she slowly moved across the room. Her small curvy hips slightly moved from side to side. Her breast appeared as small melons lying in an open field, awaiting to be picked. Her lips were as beautiful as a red rose and sweeter than honey. Her eyes sparkled like that of a diamond upon a hill that was just within reach of my outstretched hand . Her cheeks shone as bright as a silky pink rose blooming in the early morning light. Her beauty could no man claim for his own, except for him in whom she had chosen to entrust with the key to her heart.

"Well hello, Jimi. It's been a long time since I've seen you. How have you been?"

"Stash, yes, it has been some time since we have seen each other. Now as for myself, I have been doing good, thank you for asking. Stash, I came by because I've heard that you've been having some problems with your heart."

"Well, Jimi, they tell me that it's nothing to be concerned about. They say there this doctor that they know who can fix the problem by doing what's called ablation."

As I was telling Jimi this, in walked Mrs. John. She asked if we would like to join her and Mr. John in the kitchen for a cup of coffee.

"Yes, Mrs. John. I would like a cup of your coffee, but I can't speak for Stash."

"No, Jimi, you can't at that. He doesn't need asking. It can be hundred and one degrees out and he would have a cup in his hand."

"Now, Stash, as John and I were reading over your notes for your new book, I noticed that you had written a letter home. May I ask, is this a letter that you wrote and didn't send home?"

AROUND THE COFFEE TABLE

"**M**RS. MARY, THAT LETTER CAME to my mind while I was sitting all alone at the ocean today. I was thinking back on that time so long ago in my life. It was the first time, but not the last, that I would find myself to be separated from my beautiful, adorable wife. We had only been married two months before I had to leave for my first deployment to the Middle East. Leaving her was the hardest thing I've ever done (Hmm, wait a minute. That's outside of leaving my dog, of course). I must say going off to war was not my ideal way of starting our life together, and thinking about our friend who left this life at a young age got me wondering what I would have said in my last letter home to my family and friends knowing with each passing day, I could be the one who wouldn't return home from this war."

"Well, Stash, I know it can be a hard letter for someone to write to their family, not knowing from one day to the next what to expect when faced with an evil adversary, who has no regard for human life. I have heard that he was one of the evilest dictators who would kill his own people if they didn't obey his commands. I also heard that he even killed some of his military leaders for not agreeing with him. Stash, are you going to share more stories of your time in the military?"

"Yes, Mrs. Mary. But before I do, there is something I would like to talk to you about. You said a few weeks back that there is more to a born-again Christian than just believing."

"Yes, I remember, Stash. What I was referring to is this. I've heard all my life that there are several different ways of fasting. Like for instance, going without watching TV or having no power to run their air conditioner for a week or reading the newspaper, etc. The material things of this world which has no spiritual values behind them, and there are those who say, 'Once saved, always saved.' For I believe there is only one true way to fast and that is to go without food and water like Jesus did. For his disciples one day asked him, 'Master, how to do we receive such power: and Jesus answered them by pray and fasting.'

> Moreover, when ye fast, be not, as the hypocrites, of a sad countenance: for they disfigure their faces, that they may appear unto men to fast. Verily I say unto you, they have their reward. But thou, when thou fastest, anoint thine head, and wash thy face; That thou appear not unto men to fast, but unto thy Father which is in secret: and thy Father, which seeth in secret, shall reward thee openly. (Matt. 6:16–18, KJV)

"Now as for 'once save, always saved,' Son, looking back to the scriptures where Jesus speaks this parable about a man, whose house was once cleaned but once again became filled with sin, I'm looking at this from a spiritual standpoint. The house represents the body in which the spirit lives, for Jesus does refer more than once to the body as being the temple. Now reading the book of Luke, Jesus had this to say:

> When the unclean spirit is gone out of a man, he walketh through dry places, seeking rest; and finding none, he said, I will return unto my house whence came out. and when he cometh, he findeth it swept and garnished. Then goeth he, and taketh to him seven other spirits more wicked than himself; and they enter in, and dwell there: and the last state of that man is worse than the first. (Luke 11:24)

"Now, son, you may not understand these scriptures that I just shared with you if a newborn Christian, who has accepted Jesus as their personal savior, doesn't receive the right nurturing in which they need to grow spiritually. They will more likely return from which they came and become more wicked. Do you remember the parable about the prodigal son who was safe in his father's house until he ended up in the pigpen? Now I'm looking at this in the spiritual rim to say that he was once saved until he ended up living in the pigpen, the world of sin. If he hadn't realized this and repented, he would had died in sin. Let me show you this in the book of Revelation:

> He that overcometh, the same shall be clothed in
> white raiment; and I will not blot out his name out
> of the book of life, but I will confess his name before
> my Father, and before his angels. (Rev. 3:5, KJV)

As I was listening to her read, my eyes caught a glimpse of Jimi's peachy cheeks and her beautiful red lips as she sipped her coffee. Oh, how I—"

"Son, are you even listening to what I'm saying here?"

"No, Mary, he's not. He has his eyes glued on Jimi."

"Now, John, you old goat, you need to mind your own business."

"Yes, Ms. Mary, I was listening. And if you don't mind me saying, there are people who are going to say that you're just taking certain scriptures from the Bible to fit your own beliefs even though you're reading the scriptures as written. You know, without spiritual conviction, there's no repentance. And without repentance, one has no salvation. Now take David for instance. If he hadn't been brought under conviction by Nathan who God sent to reprimand him of his sin, which was committing adultery with Bathsheba, who was the wife of another man. If he had not had a spiritual conviction, he may not have ever repented. For there are some who would say that Jesus was not born at the time David committed his adultery. Therefore, he was not covered by the blood and didn't need to repent."

"Yes, son, and that's why I would like to share this from the book of Philippians with you:

> Wherefore, my beloved, as ye have always obeyed, not
> as in my presence only, but now much more in my

absence, work out your own salvation with fear and
trembling. For it is God which worketh in you both to
will and to do of his good pleasure. (Phil. 2:12 KJV)

"Ms. Mary, I have enjoyed the coffee and conversation, but I
must be on my way home before it gets too late."

"Jimi, it has been an honor to have you in our home. You're
always welcome here."

"Thank you, Ms. Mary."

"Yes, Jimi, please stop by anytime. You know Son loves having
you around."

"John, once again, you need to mind your own business."

"Jimi, if you don't mind, I'll walk you home."

"Son, I don't mind at all. I was hoping you would as there is
something I would like to talk with you about."

"Ms. Mary, if you don't mind, we can work on the book when
I get back from seeing Jimi home, okay?"

"Sure, son. That'll give me time to look over what you have
already written."

* * * * *

"Now, Jimi, what did you want to talk with me about?"

"Son, it's nothing important. I just didn't want to walk back all
alone. Oh, have you heard that Mr. Mack's third wife had twins last
week."

"Now, Jimi, you know I don't get down this way anymore now
that you have taken up with his young son."

"Well, she had a boy and girl. The boy looks just like Mr. Mack
when he was a baby, and she looks like her mom. Are you coming in
to see them?"

"No, Jimi. I must be getting back. It has truly been great seeing
you again. May I give you a good- night kiss?" *Oh, only if I could find
the words to win your heart, Jimi. Only if you knew how my love for
you burns deep within my soul. Just caressing your sweet lips with mine
would melt me to my knees.*

"Well, son, I was beginning to wonder if you were ever going to ask, but I must say no. I'm engaged to married now. Thank you for walking me home tonight. It brought back some great memory of when we first came to this town."

"Well, it did for me also, Jimi, and I'm so sorry that we must say good night for the last time."

"Son, wait. There is one more thing I would like to tell of you."

"Yes, Jimi, what's on your mind?"

"Well, son, you said you don't get down this way anymore now that I'm with my fiancée."

"Jimi, please don't. There is nothing to explain. What you do from here on is your own business."

"Son, I'm sorry you feel that way. I was hoping that you would be happy for me. You're a very sweet man, and I'm hoping one day you will find the right woman who is going to make you forget all about me."

"Well, Jimi, thank you for your kind words, but I don't think that there's another woman in this world who can ever make me forget about you, for your kind heart can never be replaced by any woman."

A SAD WALK HOME

Now that Jimi has found the love of her life, I once again found myself to be alone in this desolate desert as it appeared. I must say this has been quite a journey which I've found myself to be on. But now I needed to be moving on in order to find my one true love. Well, that was if she even existed out there somewhere in this big old world. But just where would I even begin to look. I'm feeling as lost today as I did when I first began this search for her over these past five years, but who knows, only time would tell.

My dearest Jimi, as I walked you home last night, I found myself thinking back to the first time I laid my eyes upon you. Only if I could find the words to tell you how your beauty alone made me feel as if I've died in this old desert in which we have found ourselves to be in. Looking upon your face, I felt as if I was looking into the eyes of an angel. All the time that I've spent trying to find ways to win your heart, Jimi, you went and gave it over to another man whom you know little about.

This farewell letter was not coming out right.

As I walked in the house, Mr. and Mrs. John was sitting in the living room. I asked Mrs. John, "Where's my notebook? There are some things I need to write down while they're still on my mind."

"Son, it's lying on the kitchen table right where you left it."

"Okay, thanks, got it. But before we get started, I would like a cup of coffee. Would you like one as well?"

"No, thank you, son. Let's get started on your stories."

"Okay, Ms. Mary. After returning home from this deployment to the Middle East, the unit would once again find themselves to be reorganized, becoming known as a detachment company. Being a small entity of the 3656th maintenance company, we had to be trained in a new MOS. Having multiple MOS's meant one thing, that the military could call upon you individually to serve wherever they may need you. Now being the detachment. and not the company, we had been assigned this new second lieutenant as our commander. He was a graduate from the Reserve Officers Training Corp (ROTC) and was fresh as a newborn. Hmm!

"Now there was this one year that Det. got called to go out to a National Training Center (NTC) in support of the training unit's rotation. Upon arriving at NTC, we sat up in a low-lying area located at the foot of the mountains."

"Stash, why did y'all sat up at the foot of the mountains?"

"Well, John, that's where they put us. And let me say when it rained, that place would become flooded from the water running down from the mountains. We filled sandbags and placed them around our tent to help keep the water from flooding the tent. Although by doing this, the water could back up around our generator. We lost the generator due to the flood. Within the next day or so, we received a mission to haul some supplies to where the training unit was for their training. Now our new second lieutenant was leading the convoy out, and somewhere along the way, he took the wrong turn and ended up right in the middle of the training event that was taking place between the training unit and the opposing force. There were tanks coming from both sides and planes flying over, dropping flares."

"What did y'all do, Stash?"

"Well, John, we stopped the convoy only long enough to find out just what was going on before moving on to our destination."

"What did y'all do next, Son?"

"Well, John, our next mission was to haul ammunition from the ammo dump out to the training unit for their gunnery exercise. We were told that this mission was going to be a turn and burn. Well, it didn't go as planned. We ended up spending the night out there with no food or water, no sleeping bags, and no change of clothes. I ended up sleeping in the cab of the truck, and two of my friends slept on the trailer. Now this was the first time, but not the last time, that we would find ourselves sleeping under the stars. As time went on, we went out on another mission with this first lieutenant who got us lost out in the middle of the desert, and we ended up spending the night on the side of the mountains. Now what can one say about these new young lieutenant; who went on to become among the finest officers with whom I've had the pleasure of serving under their command. Now as the years continued to move on, so did I. I went on to become a member of another unit, water purification company, up in the northern part of the state.

"There are so many great stories about this unit that I could tell you, but time is not on my side, so I'm only going to share what I consider to be among the funniest ones."

"Okay, son, just tell me your stories. Ms. Mary and I be the judges if they are funny or not."

"Mr. John, your smart comments are the very reason I'm only going to share a few more stories and then I'm gone."

"Whatever do you mean you're gone?"

"Well, tonight, as I walked Jimi home, I could see it in her eyes that she has found the love of her life. Therefore, there's no need for me to hang around here any longer."

"Son, I'm so sorry. I was hoping that you would find some way to win the key to her heart."

"Well, Ms. Mary, thank you. But there is no hope of that ever happening. Now can we just get back to my stories?"

"Son, I understand that you don't want to talk about her any longer."

"Thanks, Ms. Mary. Now before I get too far off track, I was talking about my time with the unit up north. The unit got their mobilization orders to serve overseas. Before moving to the training site for our training, we had to pack the equipment. During this time, we had some visitors who stopped by to see how things were going. One of them said that he had heard about this old cotton gin off Interstate 82 that someone had turned into a restaurant called Bourbon Mall and would like to check it out. When we got off that night, we loaded up the van, and off we went. Well, when it came time to head back, guess who got asked to drive back? Hmm, yes, me). Now you got to understand this was my first or second time of ever going to this place, and I didn't know my way around all that well. And of all things, the van had only one headlight working. It was like trying to drive with someone sitting on the hood holding a candle. But that's beside the point, right? So off we went. Guess who, of all people, was sitting behind me. He was the worst backseat driver. If there's ever been one, he was it."

"Now, son, he couldn't have been that bad."

"John, I tell you. I just wanted to put him out on the hood holding another candle. We finally got to end of the road, and I asked which way should I go. They said to go left, so I went left, and all at once, they started screaming, 'You're going the wrong way.'

"I asked, 'How? You all said go left.'

"They replied, 'Yes, but over on the other side of the interstate.'

"Now after the unit had left for the Middle East, I ended up on medical hold at another base for three or four months. After returning home from medical hold, I was assigned to the rear detachment, which was at the time located at a different location from the base unit. Now our acting first sergeant asked if I would be interested in going with two other service members to train on a new system. This system had been modified for larger capacity production. We went back home a week or so before drill weekend. Now first sergeant didn't inform us until we were on our way to drill that we were going to have some visitors who were interested in seeing the new system setup in an operation, and that myself and the other two persons would have to explain how the system works. We got the system set up for show. The visitors have now arrived, and my heart began to beat faster than normal."

"Wait now, son. Just why was your heart beating faster than normal?"

"John, I've only once, in my entire career, briefed a two-star general, and that was when I was only a PFC. I finished my part of the class and said, 'Sir, I'm so sorry for not knowing ahead of time that you were coming, or I would've been better prepared. But the

FS didn't tell us until we were on our way here." They turned and looked at the FS, and he in return looked at me and said, 'Thanks forthrowing me under the bus.' I didn't know until some years later that he had bragged on how well I had briefed the general.

"Now John that's all the ones I'm going to share about my time with the water purification company. There was one, or two, from my time with a logistics unit that I would like to share before calling it done. It was around Thanksgiving, and the captain wanted to have a half marathon run. He had tasked me and three other people to mark the route. Well, I forgot the tape needed to tape the turkeys to the mile markers. I went back in the office and picked up a roll, and on my way back to the truck, I was trying to find the end of it. I was getting frustrated. I did a drop kick and missed it, and started dancing around on one leg like a chicken with its head cut off. Two of my buddies started laughing and almost fell out of the truck."

"Son, are you going to tell us about the locked door that you mentioned earlier?"

"Okay, John. One more and then I'm done. I was working in the mayor's office at this base in Afghanistan when I got an opportunity to go with a buddy to visit another base. They put us in the temporary housing. Now, John, just to let you know, I don't sleep well in an unfamiliar location. We had talked at the unit at 2:30 a.m. or so that night, before going bed. Now after being in bed for about thirty to forty-five minutes, I had to go to the outhouse."

"What! I know you didn't just say the outhouse."

"Yes, John, I did."

"Well, son, I'm going to get a cup of coffee. Would you like a cup?"

"No, John, I'm trying to tell my story about the locked door. Now do you want to hear it or not?"

"No, son, not if it has anything to do with the outhouse."

"No, John, it does not have anything to do with the outhouse. It's what took place afterward that got me."

"Well, okay. Go ahead. I'll wait for the coffee."

"Thank you. Now as I was saying, I had to go to the outhouse. I went and returned to the room. The door handle broke in my hand, and I couldn't get back in. I didn't know what I was going to do to get back in the room. I was sure that my buddy was asleep, and I didn't want to wake him, knowing he had a loaded weapon by his bed."

"Son, just why would your friend have a loaded weapon?"

"John, we were in an unsecured location in Afghanistan. Now that's my story about the locked door."

"Son, I didn't see anything funny at all about that story."

"No, John. I didn't think that you would. Now will there be anything else before I go?"

"No. I don't know of anything."

FAREWELL LETTER

My Dearest Jimi,

I AM WRITING YOU THIS LETTER because I want you to know from the first time I saw your sweet innocent smile, my heart went into a deep longing desire for a love such as yours. I knew then my heart could go on beating for eternity. All the times that we have spent together have been among the best times of my life. The walks we took down by the ocean in the moonlight will live forever in my heart. There this one night I recall, we took a walk down by the ocean. You had sung this song that was one of the most amazing songs my ears have ever heard. You told me it was a song that your mom had taught you as a young girl and that you have always dreamed of one day taking a walk down by the ocean in the moonlight and sing it in memory of her.

She must have been one special lady, but then again, all moms are special. Then there's the memory of us riding back to your father's mansion on the back of a camel, and I laid my head upon your shoulder, covering my face with your autumn hair. I still remember it having the smell of coconut milk, and then there was the night around the campfire as we made our way here to this town. Only if I had known that by coming to this little town you would fall in love with another man, I would have went another way. For the memories we had made together over the past year and half will in no time find themselves to become only a lonely memory that will live only in my heart.

Just like the red and yellow roses and the note I wrote just for you, I was hoping they would be the beginning of the pathway that would lead me to find the key to your heart, but I'm guessing they weren't good enough for a woman like yourself. I feel I'd be lying to you and myself if I were to say I didn't have some feelings for you. I'm sure like you said last night when we were standing outside of your new love home, they will one day fade like a fading heartbeat. With this being said, I want you to know that I'm very happy for you, and

I do hope nothing but the best for you and your new love as you both start your lives together as one. I don't know just where this old road may take me in life, but I hope it will lead me to someone like you, who has always but God and their family first. I can only hope that you will always hold our memories as close to your heart as I will.

Jimi, I don't know what else to say other than it has been a great journey getting to know you, but now the time has come for me to say farewell for the last time, for I must be moving on to begin a new chapter in my life.

P.S. If we never see each other again on this side of God's beautiful world, just know my love will always be with you in spirit.

Love,
Son

AN UNKNOWN ROAD

THE DAY HAS COME FOR me to leave. As I made my way down the hall, I heard Mr. and Mrs. John talking in the kitchen. I thought to myself, "How I'm going to miss these two. They have become like my mom and dad. They've been so kind to me since I've been here."

I walked into the room and handed Mrs. John the letter and asked her to give it to Jimi after I have left. Mr. John looked over and asked me, "Just where are you planning on going, Son?"

I replied, "Mr. John, I don't know. I am guessing wherever this old rugged road may take me."

"Son, you know we will miss having you here with us."

"Yes, Mrs. John, I know, and I'm going to miss you all as well. But this is something I must do now that she is engaged to you-know-who, so please see that she gets this."

"Son, you know I will, and you better drop us a line or two when you get to where you are going or whenever you can."

"Okay, Mrs. John, I will."

* * * * *

"John, I hope that he's going to be okay out there all alone."
"Mary, he's going to be okay. Now let's see what's in the letter."

"No, John, you are not reading this letter. It's for Jimi. I'm going to take it over to her right now."

* * * * *

"Good afternoon, Jimi. How are you today?"

"Hello, Ms. Mary. I'm doing well, thank you."

"Jimi, I hope you don't mind me stopping by without calling first, but there is something that I thought you should hear from me first. Son has left. He said he needed to start a new chapter in his life and asked if I would see that you get this."

"Ms. Mary, did he say where he was going?"

"No. All he said was wherever the road may take him."

"Ms. Mary, thank you for letting me know and for bringing this by as well."

"Jimi, I must be getting back before John checks the mail. I had ordered him one of Son's books over a month ago. It should be here by now."

"Okay, Ms. Mary. You be careful on your way home. And once again, thanks for bringing this by."

"You're very welcome."

* * * * *

"John, it's been only three hours since Son left for parts unknown, and I'm already missing him. I was hoping that his book would have gotten here before he left."

"What did you just say?"

"John, you know good and well what I said. I was hoping he could tell us more about it."

"Well, Mary, if his stories were anything like the ones he shared with us, I know that whoever did the editing portion must have fell out of the chair laughing, trying to make something out of nothing."

"Now John, someone's knocking at the door."

ABOUT THE AUTHOR

GEORGE MILLS IS THE PUBLISHED author of two other books the titles, *As the Journey Begins*, and the sequel, *Looking Forward as the Journey Continues*. He returns with his latest title, *The Footprints of an American Soldier*.

George grew up in a small community known as Mulberry, located in Wayne County. His family moved to Jones County when he was just a young boy. He started Glade Elementary School at the age of six. After his first year at Glade Elementary, his family decided to move back to Mulberry were he went on to successfully graduate from Clara High School. After graduation, he decided to try his hand at serving his country by joining his hometown National Guard Unit.

Within the pages of this book, he shares some of his unique stories while on his journey looking for his beloved wildflower to become his soul mate.